MAN OVERBOARD!

MAN OVE[RBOARD]

RBOARD!

CURTIS PARKINSON

TUNDRA BOOKS

Published in Canada by Tundra Books,
75 Sherbourne Street, Toronto, Ontario M5A 2P9

Published in the United States by Tundra Books of Northern New York,
P.O. Box 1030, Plattsburgh, New York 12901

Library of Congress Control Number: 2011923287

Library and Archives Canada Cataloguing in Publication

Parkinson, Curtis
Man overboard! / Curtis Parkinson.

ISBN 978-1-77049-298-1

I. Title.

PS8581.A76234M36 2012   jC813.'54   C2011-901382-7

We acknowledge the financial support of the Government of Canada through
the Book Publishing Industry Development Program (BPIDP) and that of the
Government of Ontario through the Ontario Media Development
Corporation's Ontario Book Initiative. We further acknowledge the support of
the Canada Council for the Arts and the Ontario Arts Council for our
publishing program.

ONTARIO ARTS COUNCIL
CONSEIL DES ARTS DE L'ONTARIO

Design: Andrew Roberts

Printed in the United States of America

1 2 3 4 5 6   17 16 15 14 13 12

To my fellow deckhands on the Rapids Prince,
way back then

JULY 1943

ONE

At a blast from the ship's horn, the lines were cast off. The *Rapids Prince* was under way. Their work done for the moment, the tired deckhands could relax.

All except Scott.

No. Not when he knew who was up there, mixing with the other passengers, acting as if they were just tourists too. German agents, Scott suspected, from what he'd overheard – one could be the agent rumored to have landed recently from a U-boat on the East Coast, the other already established in the country.

Yet he couldn't tell anybody, especially not the captain, because of what he'd been up to when he happened to overhear them. Knowing the captain's temper, he'd be fired on the spot. So would his friend Adam.

It was just so frustrating. All Scott could do was wait and try to figure out what those two were up to. They must have had a reason for boarding the *Rapids Prince* – surely not for the rapids, thrilling as they were, or the scenery. And there were quicker ways to get to Montreal. They could have been driven there in their Packard, on the King's Highway 2, in three hours, whereas the *Rapids Prince* took most of the day. So why were they there, mingling with the genuine tourists?

He sighed. There was nothing he could do about it. He might as well join his fellow deckhands, who were clustering around the access doorway on the lower deck to watch the rapids. For shooting the Long Sault was a thrilling ride, no matter how many times you'd done it before.

As the ship entered the rapids, it began to pick up speed, like a roller coaster starting on its downhill run. And it really was a run. The St. Lawrence River, Scott had read somewhere, drains an eighth of the continent, and all that water is squeezed – tumbling, twisting, and turning – into one narrow gap, creating the Long Sault Rapids.

Mere feet away, a giant wave swept by, sunlight glinting on its surface. So close yet so far, provided the pilot stayed within the narrow channel that represented safety.

On the deck above, passengers lined the rails. A man wielding one of the new-fangled movie cameras was calling instructions to his children, who obstinately refused to smile. A lady nearby pulled her young son down from the rail he'd been climbing. Only a soldier and his bride, the confetti still in her hair, stared into each other's eyes, ignoring the rapids. It looked like the war would keep them apart for years yet. . . .

Up in the wheelhouse, Captain Plum was pacing. He'd made this run almost five hundred times, yet he could never stop worrying. The pilot at the wheel knew the route through the rapids like the back of his hand, and the ship was especially designed for the task. Yet the captain continued to worry.

A sturdy three-decker, the *Rapids Prince* had the shallow draft necessary to navigate the rapids. It also had lots of deck space for viewing the rapids and a fine dining room to keep the tourists happy for the day-long trip to Montreal.

Yet the thought of those rocks flashing by, rocks that could rip a gash in the hull of his precious ship, kept the captain tense. He felt in his pocket for an antacid. His ulcer always acted up on excursion days.

Beside him, the pilot gripped the wheel tightly, his eyes peering ahead for the landmarks only he was privy to – a certain pine tree on a point of land, a painted barn on the starboard shore. Landmarks he would use to guide the *Rapids Prince* safely past the rocks; landmarks learned from the Indians centuries ago and passed along within the pilot's family for generations. It was rumored that Lloyds of London's insurance on the vessel was valid only if a pilot from this particular family was at the helm.

"Here we go," one of the deckhands exclaimed. "It's the maelstrom coming up!" The maelstrom was where the turbulence reached its peak.

Then, suddenly, from the deck above, someone screamed.

The scream was followed by a shout: "Man overboard!"

TWO

It was bedlam. The passengers rushed to the stern. The first mate grabbed a life ring and pushed through the crowd. "Make way, make way!"

He could see no sign of anyone, but he threw the ring in the unlikely event whoever had gone overboard had surfaced. Immediately seized by the churning water, the life ring disappeared.

On the bridge, Captain Plum's first thought was to signal the engine room to reverse, but he dared not risk it in the rapids. All he could do was reach up and blow six short blasts on the ship's whistle – the MAN OVERBOARD signal. By this time, though, most passengers already knew.

The pilot at the wheel, distracted by the commotion, missed a crucial landmark, and the ship strayed ever so slightly off course. That was all it took. The

Rapids Prince gave a lurch, like a building in an earthquake, then shook herself, straightened up, and kept going.

Captain Plum knew instantly what that lurch meant. It was what he'd feared most. His ship had grazed one of those deadly rocks. He groaned. The loss of a passenger overboard in the rapids was enough of a calamity; add an encounter with a rock and it became a catastrophe.

Scott and the other deckhands had heard the shouts from the deck above and felt the lurch of the ship a moment later. Stunned, the inexperienced deckhands looked at each other. *We should do something, shouldn't we? But what exactly?*

Some wanted to rush up top and ready a lifeboat, but on a passenger run they had strict instructions to stay out of the way unless they were summoned by the first mate. So they waited.

Scott stared out at the raging torrent as the *Rapids Prince* plunged on. Whoever it was who'd gone overboard didn't stand a chance. *Did those two suspected German agents on the deck above have anything to do with it? Or is it a coincidence that this happened when they were aboard? And that lurch? Did we graze one of those deadly rocks? Are we in danger of sinking?* He felt inadequate, so new on the job that he had no idea what to do, except wait for orders.

The ship's speed slowed as she entered calmer water below the rapids. Finally it was safe for the captain to signal for reverse; the propellers churned, and the ship came to a gradual halt.

The deckhands were summoned then, and a lifeboat was lowered. Two manned the oars and a third was posted in the bow as a lookout. The first mate sat in the stern and barked out orders, reminding Scott of Captain Bligh in the movie *Mutiny on the Bounty*.

Captain Plum radioed the nearest police patrol and reported the man overboard. He then turned to the pilot and advised him that the ship would not proceed one inch farther until the extent of the damage from the rock was assessed by the chief engineer. Accordingly, the pilot selected a tree on the nearby shore, where he judged the water to be deep enough, and maneuvered the ship as close to the bank as he dared.

A rope was rigged at the end of a long hinged boom to bridge the ten-foot gap between the ship and the bank. The second mate beckoned to Scott and handed him the rope. "Off you go, then."

Scott grasped the rope and shoved off. The boom swung out, but not quite far enough to reach the shore. He was left dangling high over the water, kicking like a puppet on a string. From the deck above, he heard titters from the passengers at the rail.

The boom, with Scott still hanging on, was hauled back in for a second try. This time he gave a mighty shove off, the boom swung out all the way, and he dropped onto the grassy bank. A scattering of applause came from the passengers, and he began to feel like a sideshow diverting their attention from the tragedy of the man overboard.

Mooring lines were thrown to him, and Scott secured the ship fore and aft to sturdy pine trees. Then he sat down on the grassy bank to await orders.

Surveying the passengers gathered at the rail, he didn't see any sign of the men he suspected of being German agents among them. He did, however, spot his girlfriend, Lindsay, with her mother and father. Conscious of the watching crowd, he gave her a tentative wave, hoping she hadn't seen him dangling helplessly from the boom.

He'd been pining for her ever since he'd left home for his summer job, and now, when he saw her so close, his heart beat faster.

Lindsay smiled and waved back. A boy stood beside her at the rail, and Scott saw, to his annoyance, that it was Ian Day from their high school. Ian was six foot two, popular with the girls, and president of the student council.

Scott watched jealously as Ian leaned over and said

something to Lindsay that made her laugh. *The creep is probably making fun of me.* He plucked a blade of grass to chew on. Now Ian was touching her arm. Nothing was going right today.

When the lifeboat returned, the first mate shook his head. Then it sunk home to the watchers that they were witnessing a tragedy.

The first mate delivered his report to the bridge. "Couldn't find a thing, Captain," he said. "The body may have sunk, or it may be hung up on a rock in the maelstrom."

"I'm not surprised," the captain said. "The police patrol will have to drag below the rapids, though I doubt they'll find anything. . . ."

"The crew's all accounted for," the first mate said. "Must have been a passenger. The woman who screamed told me she'd been at the rail and just happened to catch a glimpse of a body hurtling down and hitting the water with a splash. The man beside her said he'd seen a man's arm sticking up out of the water for a moment, his fingers clawing at the side, like he was trying to grab on to something. But then, he was gone."

The captain fully expected to be faced at any minute with a distraught wife, her words tumbling out about a missing husband, or a mother weeping for her child who'd fallen overboard. Yet no one appeared, no one who had even lost track of a traveling companion. It was eerie: a man overboard and no one reported missing.

He made an announcement over the loudspeaker, asking any passengers who knew of someone missing to report to the purser's office immediately. When no one appeared, he made a second announcement, asking everyone on board to have their names checked off the purser's passenger list. A lineup formed immediately outside his office.

Meanwhile, the chief engineer was busy looking for any signs of a leak from the encounter with the boulder. The captain waited impatiently for his report. He had a boatload of passengers due in Montreal tonight.

Eventually the lineup outside the purser's office dwindled to nothing, and the purser sat down to go through his list. He discovered that every passenger's name had been checked off except one – that of a certain Derek Patterson, for whom, he recalled, a reservation had been made at the last minute by phone.

"I guess it's up to the police to figure out who he is," he said. "Who he was, I mean."

"That's odd," the captain said. "A reservation for

one, made at the last minute." He stroked his chin. "Most people travel with their family or friends. But it looks like nobody on board has ever heard of this man."

But there *was* someone on board who'd heard of Derek Patterson. That someone was Scott, and he'd heard of him because of the conversation he'd overheard that morning, when he was on the running board of the Packard eating pie instead of working.

But he wasn't about to admit that to anyone, especially not the captain.

THREE

When Scott first saw the car pull up alongside the ship earlier that day, it had taken his breath away. A Packard Twelve Touring Sedan, with a uniformed chauffeur up front. *What a beauty!* Just like the one in the full-page glossy magazine ads he used to clip out before the war – when they were still making cars instead of tanks. But he'd never imagined he'd get the chance to see one up close.

The Packard Twelve Touring Sedan had a powerful twelve-cylinder engine under its long hood, whitewalls, fancy chrome wings as a hood ornament, a luxurious backseat of Moroccan leather, a built-in bar with crystal decanters, and a speaking-tube to communicate with the chauffeur up front. He couldn't make out who was in the back of this one, but he figured it must be someone important or rich.

The chauffeur had jumped out to open the back door, and Scott had waited to see who emerged. One thing he knew: it wouldn't be the prime minister. A Packard Twelve Touring Sedan wasn't dull old Mackenzie King's sort of thing. But it could be someone famous – some movie star even, like Rita Hayworth or Jimmy Cagney!

However, when the actual owner did step out, he sure didn't look like a movie star. More like some wealthy but boring businessman. He wore a gray double-breasted suit and matching fedora, and the shine on his shoes was so bright it reflected the sun. "Park it," he ordered the chauffeur.

Scott watched him stride up the gangway, where the ship's purser stood, haughtily wielding a clipboard.

"Dale is the name," the man said, reaching in his pocket and casually peeling several bills from a fat bankroll. "G. Phillip Dale."

The purser's attitude changed instantly from haughty to subservient. "Welcome aboard the *Rapids Prince*, Mr. Dale," he purred, ticking off the name on his clipboard. "Anything I can do to make your trip more enjoyable, you have only to ask."

"I'll tell you exactly what you can do," the man said. "I'm a person who likes to keep his affairs private. You can forget you ever saw me. Or my chauffeur, Twitch."

"I've already forgotten," the purser said, smoothly pocketing the bills.

Why would the man in the gray suit want to travel alone on the Rapids Prince, *his only company a couple of hundred tourists, and why would he want the purser to forget he'd ever seen him or his chauffeur?* Scott wondered.

But he could see the second mate looking for him, so he needed to stop speculating and get back to work. There was still plenty for the deckhands to do before the *Rapids Prince* was ready to cast off.

The chauffeur, meanwhile, had parked the car, then he too boarded the ship, but using the crew's gangway to the lower deck. "I'm looking for the washroom," he said curtly to a deckhand, who pointed out the crew's washroom to him.

When Scott saw the chauffeur, he gathered up his courage. "Excuse me . . ." he began.

The chauffeur stopped and stared at him.

Scott took a deep breath. "Would it be all right if I had a look at your car, sir? I've never seen a Packard Twelve before – a real one, I mean, not just a picture." He hesitated, intimidated by the hostile stare.

"Get lost, kid," the chauffeur snarled. "And stay away from that car."

Just then, someone accidentally dropped a wrench

on the metal deck with a loud clang, and the chauffeur jumped as if he'd been shot. He slumped away, his chin twitching violently.

"Shell-shocked in the First World War, I'll wager," Bert, the veteran helmsman, commented. "I had a buddy like that. The shelling got to him. They accused him of cowardice and told him he was lucky he wasn't shot for desertion. That's what they did back then."

"I heard his boss refer to him as Twitch," a deckhand said. "Now I know why."

"Poor guy," Bert said. "It's not right. These days, they call it battle fatigue, not shell shock, and it can happen to anyone. They shouldn't make fun of it."

As Scott was taking this in, his friend Adam, a waiter, came by to slip him word that there was apple pie on the menu today. "Just thought you'd be interested," he whispered with a wink. "Come up in ten minutes and wait outside the dining room."

"*Psst*, over here! Take it, quick, before someone sees you."

Scott edged along the deck and grabbed the plate held out to him by a seemingly disembodied hand – the person behind the hand being shielded by the whitewashed bulkhead.

"Got it. Thanks, Adam."

The hand disappeared, and Scott heard Adam calling out a new order to the kitchen. "Two apple pie and one caramel pudding." This time it was a legitimate order for the table Adam was serving, not a bogus order for a friend.

Scott smiled. *That Adam.* He, Scott, could never pull that off. He'd never make a waiter in the first place, even though waiters were rewarded with generous tips from the vacationing tourists. But Adam, with his quick wit and ready memory, was good at it. Being a deckhand still suited Scott just fine.

Carefully keeping the plate level so the ice cream on top of the pie, melting rapidly in the July heat, wouldn't slide off, he scooted down the metal stairs to the lower deck where the deckhands stayed. He weaved through the piles of ropes and fenders, looking for a secluded place to sit and enjoy his pie unobserved. But there was nowhere he wouldn't be seen by the second mate, who was still hanging around.

Then Scott had a brilliant idea. *The Packard. Of course!* It was parked in the shade of maple trees on the grass fringe alongside the pier, with the side blinds pulled down. He'd seen both the owner and the chauffeur come aboard earlier, so no one would be in it. He could eat his pie on the running board, shielded from view by the trees and by the bulk of the car, then he could have a close-up look at the gleaming Packard, and no one the wiser. Two birds with one stone.

And he'd be back in lots of time to finish up his chores before the ship was due to cast off.

FOUR

Pie in hand, Scott slipped down the gangway and around to the far side of the Packard, where he perched on its shelflike running board. The nicely browned crust and the golden yellow apples made his mouth water in anticipation.

The ship's passengers got the best of everything. Naturally, they paid enough for it. In the crew's mess, however, the deckhands got only the leftovers – it would be dried-out caramel pudding for them tonight, not a whiff of apple pie à la mode.

Scott had just picked up the fork Adam had thoughtfully provided and was digging in when he heard a voice nearby. He started guiltily and looked around, but saw no one. Then he heard it again – smooth yet ominously sinister – and he realized, with a sinking feeling, that it was coming from the backseat of the car, behind the blinds.

The man in the gray suit must have come back to his car for something. He was now separated from Scott by only the thickness of a car door!

Scott scrunched down on the running board.

"I want you to get this right, no foul-ups," the voice said. "Got that?"

A second voice responded. "Got it, Mr. Vandam," and Scott recognized the voice of the surly chauffeur.

He looked around anxiously. *Can I get back to the ship without them seeing me?*

"I'll go over it just once more," the first voice continued, "so listen carefully. We stay in the car until Heinrik gets here on the *Kingston,* then he and I will board the *Rapids Prince* so he can have a look at the layout on the way to Montreal. He's our explosives expert."

The *Kingston,* the sister ship of the *Rapids Prince,* was due any minute. A paddle wheeler, too big to tackle the rapids, the *Kingston* made a regular overnight run from Toronto, along Lake Ontario and the Thousand Islands, to Prescott, where its passengers transferred to the much smaller *Rapids Prince* for the trip through the rapids to Montreal.

"Heinrik's alerted me that he's being followed," Vandam said. "He thinks it's a government agent and suspects the man's been on his trail since he landed."

Scott was riveted. He stayed absolutely still, listening intently.

"Heinrik and I will deal with him on the *Rapids Prince*. Meanwhile, you drive back to Montreal and wait for us at Victoria Pier, ready to make a fast getaway. Got that?"

"Got it, Mr. Vandam."

"And take good care of my briefcase. I don't want to carry it on board. There's top secret documents in there, with orders from the homeland."

Secret documents? Homeland? Who are these guys?

The blast of a ship's horn made Scott jump. The *Kingston* was arriving, and he realized he'd better get out of there fast before he was discovered.

"This suspected government agent," the man called Vandam was saying as Scott slid off the running board, "Heinrik's discovered his name. It's Derek Patter . . ."

The voice faded away as Scott scuttled off on all fours, like a crab chased by a hungry gull. But he'd gone only a short distance when he realized he'd forgotten the plate and fork. He'd been so flustered, he'd left them sitting on the Packard's running board. A dead giveaway. He crept back and reached out to snatch them, but they slipped from his grasp and fell on a rock with a clang.

He ran for the shelter of the ship as the car door jerked open and the man in the gray suit stepped out. The man stared down at the plate, then up at the boy running for the ship.

"Hey, you!" he yelled, but Scott kept going. "Damn kid. What was he doing here anyway, eavesdropping?"

"I'll go grab him," the chauffeur said. He started after Scott, but Vandam called him back. "Not now. Heinrik will be here any minute."

"But he could have heard everything you said, boss," the chauffeur said.

Vandam turned his icy stare on the lower deck, where Scott had disappeared. "Yeah, but he's not going anywhere; we'll take care of him later. When you meet us with the car at Victoria Pier, here's what we'll do. . . ."

Scott didn't stop until he reached the upper deck. Yanking open the door to a small storeroom, he squeezed in among the collection of mops, brooms, and buckets. He stood there in the dark, panting, and thought back to the conversation he'd overheard.

Someone called Heinrik was coming, and he and the man in the gray suit would deal with the government agent who was following him, whatever "deal with" meant. His mind flew to the rumors of a

German agent landing from a submarine in the Gulf of St. Lawrence. *Could it have been Heinrik?*

And this Vandam – who told the purser his name was G. Phillip Dale – also said they were boarding the *Rapids Prince* so Heinrik, an explosives expert, could have a look at it. *Are they planning to blow up the ship? Why would they want to blow up a boat full of tourists?* It didn't make sense. The *Rapids Prince* didn't carry war supplies. *So what is it all about?*

When Scott got his breath back, he went below where the deckhands were, to be out of sight when this Vandam and Heinrik came aboard. But he couldn't stop thinking about them.

Should he tell someone what he'd heard? He had no proof of anything, just a suspicion. Maybe he was being carried away by the rumor of an enemy agent landing from a U-boat. A rumor many scoffed at.

Meanwhile, he knew the captain was prowling around – as he did before each trip through the rapids – checking that everything was shipshape. He'd better get back to work. Scott knew the captain's temper. He'd not been on the receiving end yet, since joining the *Rapids Prince,* but his friend Adam certainly had. Adam, unfortunately, had a way of antagonizing the captain.

———

Like Scott and Adam, most of the crew on the *Rapids Prince* were high school students, working for the summer. Before the war, these jobs would have been jealously guarded by men who'd return to the *Rapids Prince* year after year. Low-paying, with long hours and hard work, the jobs had been almost impossible to come by in the Dirty Thirties.

But times had changed with the war, almost overnight, and those men were either in the armed forces now or earning better money in a war plant. Consequently, Captain Plum had to recruit sixteen- and seventeen-year-olds from high schools, many of whom were itching to join up too, as soon as they were of age. Sixteen-year-old Scott had two more years to wait. Captain Plum could only hope that a few of them, at least, would turn out to be capable seamen as the summer wore on.

Scott had heard about the job from a boy in his class who'd worked on the *Rapids Prince* the summer before. A job on a ship sounded far more interesting than packing groceries in a local store! It had a romantic ring to it. He'd tried to talk his friend Adam into applying with him.

"A sailor?" Adam had said. "I know absolutely nothing about boats."

"Ships," Scott corrected. "If it carries passengers, like the *Rapids Prince,* it's called a ship." It was one of the few times he'd been able to tell Adam something he didn't know.

"Boat, ship, whatever," Adam said. "What would the job be?"

"Deckhand," Scott said. "Sixty bucks a month and meals."

"Plus tips?"

"For deckhands? Are you kidding?"

"*Hmm,*" Adam said.

Eventually, Scott did manage to convince him, and they applied for jobs on the *Rapids Prince.* They were interviewed by Captain Plum, who lived in Kingston in the winter and knew Scott's father from the Rotary Club. Whether that had anything to do with it or not, Scott didn't know, but they were both duly accepted as deckhands.

In late June, as soon as school was finished, Scott and Adam had set out to hitchhike to Prescott, where the ship was docked. They joined the line of hitch-hikers on the King's Highway 2, many of whom were soldiers on leave from the army camp. Hitchhiking was a common way to travel during the war, with overcrowded trains and gas rationing.

It took awhile, but Scott and Adam eventually got a ride to Gananoque with a farmer in an old Ford pickup, then a second ride to Prescott with a hardware salesman, whose traveling job qualified him for extra gas coupons. In Prescott, they walked down to the waterfront and had their first glimpse of the ship that would be their home for the summer.

The *Rapids Prince* was a handsome one-stacker with three decks, no *Queen Mary* but sturdy and solidly built for shooting the rapids. With their kit bags over their shoulders, the boys stood on the pier looking up at the ship with apprehension.

"Well, don't just stand there like landlubbers, get yourselves on board!" a voice bawled from the bridge. It was Captain Plum, staring down at them. And so they climbed the gangway to begin their summer as sailors.

Scott took to it better than Adam. Not naturally coordinated like Scott, Adam was awkward when it came to leaping onto a dock to catch a mooring line, or clinging to a scaffold to scrub rust off the side. At night his joints were so stiff, he could barely climb into his upper bunk in the hold where the deckhands lived. Then, in his off time, he had to put up with the constant horseplay of the other deckhands while trying to read one of the many books he'd brought.

Not being one to sit back and accept things, Adam had kept his eyes open for a chance to change jobs. When he heard that one of the experienced waiters, who'd been expected to return for the summer, hadn't shown up, he applied. With his gift for the gab and his alert mind, he turned out to be ideally suited for the waiter's job.

Scott, however, was quite content to remain a deckhand. He liked living aboard ship and hearing the stories of the older hands, like Bert the helmsman, and he'd managed to avoid making mistakes and bringing down the captain's wrath. So far.

FIVE

Now, Scott watched from his perch on the grassy bank as the chief engineer climbed to the bridge to advise Captain Plum of the extent of the damage from the ship's encounter with the rock.

"Two plates are stove in on the port side," he said, "but there's no sign of a leak. She'll be all right until we get to Montreal, but we should have a diver examine the bottom there."

"Right," Captain Plum said. "We'll get under way, then." And he gave a toot on the ship's whistle, the signal to embark.

Scott jumped up to untie the lines from the trees he had used as mooring posts. Then the lines were winched in, and he grabbed the rope hanging from the end of the boom and swung back on board.

The *Rapids Prince* was en route once again, minus

one passenger, after its ill-starred trip through the Long Sault. And everyone wondered who the unfortunate Derek Patterson was.

Scott was still debating whether he dared go to the captain to report what he'd overheard from the running board of the Packard that morning. It was all a bit hazy now, he'd been so anxious to get away. *Did I hear the name of the man the two suspected agents said they were going to "deal with" correctly? It was Derek Patterson, wasn't it?*

He imagined the captain's response if he did tell him.

"And just what were you doing on the running board of a car, young man, when you were supposed to be working on board ship?"

"I was eating apple pie à la mode, sir."

"You were what! Where did you get it?"

No, it wouldn't do. He'd just have to keep his eyes open and see if he could learn more about the two suspected German agents.

When the *Rapids Prince* finally docked at Victoria Pier in Old Montreal that Sunday, it was nine o'clock – later than usual, but still light. The office towers of the city center were silhouetted in the distance. The passengers streaming down the gangway were boarding tour buses, cars, and taxis, anxious to get away from the tragic events of the day.

As Scott waited for Lindsay to disembark, he noticed that the Packard was parked there, with the chauffeur, Twitch, leaning nonchalantly against the hood. To Scott's relief, he didn't to seem to be paying any attention to him. He assumed he didn't recognize him as the one who had fled from the running board just that morning in Prescott. Or, if he did, he chose to forget it.

As Scott searched the crowd for Lindsay, he saw the man in the gray suit, the one who called himself G. Phillip Dale. The chauffeur had called him Mr. Vandam – whatever his name, Vandam / Dale hurried down the gangway and crossed the pier to the Packard. A few moments later, another man – younger, blond-haired, and casually dressed – disembarked and also headed for the car. *That must be the one called Heinrik,* Scott thought.

This was his last chance to learn more about them before the Packard disappeared into the city. Drifting closer, trying to appear casual, he felt tension in the air, as if something was about to happen.

The tension was broken by a shout from behind him. "Hey, Scott!" It was Adam. "Where you going?" he said. "Here comes Lindsay now."

Scott hesitated, momentarily torn. But Lindsay

was more important to him than these guys. He hurried back to greet her. At least that Ian Day wasn't with her, whispering in her ear.

Lindsay could hardly wait to tell him about the summer job she'd found as a desk clerk at the Blinkbonnie Inn. "It's just outside Prescott," she said, "and we'll be able to get together whenever the *Rapids Prince* is back in port."

"That's great news," Scott enthused. To see Lindsay every week, what a break! It was going to be a wonderful summer.

Just then Scott felt someone touch his elbow and turned to see the chauffeur, Twitch, but a far different Twitch than the one who had scowled at him that morning.

"Sorry to interrupt," he said politely. "But aren't you the one who asked me if you could take a look at the Packard when we were in Prescott?"

Scott nodded.

"Well, the boss says it would be okay if you came over now, before we leave."

It was tempting. It might be Scott's last chance to get a closer look at Vandam and Heinrik. Then at least he'd be able to describe them, if necessary, later on.

He turned to Lindsay. "Would you mind? I'll only be a few minutes."

"Go ahead," she said. "We have to wait for our luggage anyway."

"Something about this smells fishy," Adam, who'd been observing the scene, muttered to himself. He watched Scott follow the chauffeur across the pier and trailed after them.

As Scott approached the car, Vandam opened the door and beckoned to him. It seemed like a friendly gesture, yet Scott hesitated. There was something about the look in the man's eyes. . . .

Suddenly he understood. *It's a trap!*

He turned to go, but Twitch blocked his path. "No, you don't."

Adam stepped up. "What's happening, Scott?"

"Time to get out of here," he said. "Go!" Scott dodged around Twitch and started running. *But where's Adam?* When he looked back, he saw that Twitch was sprawled on top of him. Adam had stuck out a foot and tripped him up.

Twitch scrambled to his feet and started after Scott. That was when Vandam intervened. "Leave him," he ordered the chauffeur. "That one will do just as well. Grab him!"

Twitch hauled Adam to his feet, dragged him to the car, and pushed him into the backseat. Then he vaulted into the driver's seat, and the Packard took off with a screech of burning rubber.

"Adam!" Scott shouted. He raced for the car and just managed to grab hold of the luggage rack on the back. He leapt onto the bumper and hung on for dear life.

Across the pier, Lindsay and the others heard him shout and turned to look. As the car vanished into the narrow winding streets of Old Montreal, with Scott clinging to the back, they were left staring after him in bewilderment.

SIX

Scott hung on desperately as the Packard hurtled around a corner, the pavement a blur under him. He could hardly believe what he'd done; it had all happened so fast, he'd had no time to think. He'd reacted automatically to the sight of Adam being forced into the car. Now it was too late to jump off, even if he wanted to.

Another corner and the centrifugal force almost threw him off. The car charged through a stop sign, then a red light, with Scott struggling to hold on. Through the oval of the rear window, he caught a glimpse of the two men in the backseat. They were staring straight ahead and didn't seem to know he was there. The top of Adam's head was just visible, sandwiched between them.

Scott tightened his grip, ducking down below the level of the window to keep out of their sight. He heard a siren in the distance as the Packard weaved evasively through the alleys and backstreets of Old Montreal. Eventually, it faded away. All he could do was hang on.

He realized now how dangerous these men were – and they had Adam at their mercy. He should have told the captain about them. He still would, if he could get away without being collared himself.

The car sped along street after street lined with identical duplexes. There were few pedestrians about, most families at home on Sunday night. A man walking a beagle stopped and stared at Scott as the car raced by.

Finally the Packard slowed and came to a stop. Scott tensed, not sure what to do next. The street looked like all the others, lined with duplexes and not a soul in sight. If only there were more people around, he could leap off and mingle with the crowd. But, now, his best hope was to hang on and wait for an opportunity to slip away unnoticed.

The passenger door opened, and he heard someone say, "All right, out! And no funny business. One peep out of you, and you'll live to regret it."

Then the door shut and the car, unexpectedly, started to pull away. Scott glanced back and saw Vandam on the sidewalk gripping Adam, who was now blindfolded. Vandam stared after the departing car and their eyes met. "Twitch! Stop the car!" he yelled.

As the Packard screeched to a halt, Scott leapt off, looking around desperately for an escape route. Nothing but a solid line of duplexes faced him; not an alleyway in sight. He started to run up the street, but Twitch, surprisingly nimble, jumped out and blocked his way.

He turned and ran the other way, but Vandam was already there, waiting. Scott tried to dodge past him, but he reached out a long arm, grabbed his shirt, and hauled him back.

Vandam slapped him hard across the face. "Who are you, kid, some kind of paid snoop? First you're on my running board back in Prescott, now here."

Scott's cheek stung like it was on fire. He flared back, "Let my friend go!"

Vandam glanced across the road at Adam, now stumbling around on the sidewalk, disoriented. "Yeah, I figured he must be your pal when he tripped my chauffeur so you could get away. That was his big mistake. Now let me tell you something, kid."

He grabbed Scott by his shirt front and brought his face so close that Scott could smell his hot breath and feel his eyes burning into him.

"If you say one word to anyone about what you overheard this morning, your friend's life won't be worth a plugged nickel. Same thing goes if anyone shows up here looking for him. They won't find him, but I'll know who told them where to look."

He let the words sink in, then gave Scott a shake. "You got that?"

Scott, fearing for Adam's life, nodded numbly.

The man released his grip. "Okay, then, scram."

But Scott stayed stubbornly where he was. He looked over at the helpless, blindfolded Adam. "I promise not to talk if you'll let him go."

"*Ha,* you've got a lot to learn, kid," Vandam said. "That isn't the way the world works – not in wartime. Your friend will stay alive as long as you keep quiet. But if you talk . . ." he drew his hand across his throat " . . . he's a goner. Now get lost before I change my mind and get rid of the pair of you."

Scott hesitated for a second. *At least with one of us free,* he told himself, *there's a fighting chance.*

"You really gonna let him go, boss?" he heard Twitch say as he hurried away.

"Yeah, it's even better this way," Vandam said. "We got him right where we want him. As long as we hold his pal's life in our hands, he won't dare tell anybody anything." He laughed.

As Scott wandered the streets of Old Montreal, trying to find his way back to Victoria Pier, he kept telling himself that he'd agreed to his deal with the devil for Adam's sake. Discretion was supposed to be the better part of valor, wasn't it?

This was real, and Adam's life was at stake. One thing he knew for sure: he'd never forget the way the man drew his hand across his throat, suggesting Adam's fate if he, Scott, talked.

When darkness fell, there was still no sign of Victoria Pier. A pedestrian came along, and Scott stopped him to ask the way. The man shook his head, saying, «*Je ne parle pas anglais.*» But by the time Scott thought of the French words he needed, the man was gone.

In the next block, a man sitting on a step smoking a pipe listened to Scott's stumbling French and pointed down the street. «*Tout droit,*» he said, «*puis tournez à gauche.*» It took Scott a moment to figure out that that meant "straight ahead, then turn left."

He set out again, following the directions, hoping to see the familiar outline of the ship. He knew he'd be faced with a million questions. Why had he done such a risky thing, they'd want to know. How had he gotten off the speeding car without hurting himself? Where had Adam disappeared to? Why didn't they come back together? On and on. Yet he couldn't answer them without putting Adam's life in danger. Filled with dread, he almost wished he could stay lost forever.

SEVEN

Dazed by the sudden turn of events, Adam sat squeezed between the two men as the Packard raced through the streets of Old Montreal at breakneck speed. It careened around corners, with tires squealing. He had a moment of hope when he heard a siren behind them. The younger blond man took out a gun. But the siren soon faded, so he put it away and stared out at the city as if it were all new to him.

It was new to Adam, too. Urban streets flashed by. Rows and rows of attached brick duplexes that looked like they'd been built in the last century, with outside metal stairs leading up to second floors and tiny fenced yards, carefully tended, with clematis vines and rosebushes and small vegetable gardens.

The older man, on Adam's other side, produced a

bandana from a compartment and proceeded to blind-fold him.

"No need for that," Adam said. "I know nothing about Montreal. We could be in Timbuktoo." The man ignored him.

"Not so tight," Adam protested. "It's cutting off the circulation. Ease it a bit, would you?"

The only answer he got was an extra tug on the knot behind his head. "Just shut up and do what I tell you," the man said. "That way we'll get along fine, you and me."

When the Packard finally came to a stop, there wasn't a sound except the purring of its twelve-cylinder engine. "Coast is clear, boss," the chauffeur said from up front.

"I'm getting out here, Heinrik," the older man said as he opened the car door. "Twitch knows where to drop you. They're expecting you, and they'll have a birth certificate for you, in the name of Howard Taylor, and a driver's license. I'll phone you later."

"You want me to change the plates, boss?" Adam heard the chauffeur say. "Just in case."

"I don't think anyone got our license number, but why take the chance?" the boss said. "Get them to do a quick paint job, too." Then he got out and hauled Adam from the car, like he was a side of beef.

But, then, as the car pulled away, Adam heard the boss shout, "Twitch! Stop the car!" followed by a screech of tires and the slam of car doors. Some kind of commotion erupted and he was left standing on the sidewalk, unable to move for fear of tripping over something.

He heard the man's voice raised in anger. Then another voice. It sounded like Scott's! But that couldn't be. . . .

Next thing Adam knew, the boss came back and hauled him, stumbling, up a flight of metal stairs. A door opened, and he was pushed into a room smelling of onions frying.

He heard a woman's voice with a French accent say, "Philippe, is that you?" Then a gasp. "Who's this?" she said. "And why is he blindfolded?"

"Just someone for you to take care of for a while."

"No, Philippe –"

"Don't worry, he won't give you any trouble. I'll make sure of that."

"But –"

"Don't forget who's paying the rent here. You can keep him in that spare room at the end of the hall. It's got a lock on it. Where's Colette?"

"She's in her room, reading."

"She's always reading, that girl. It's not good for her – gives her ideas. Tell her to clear out the spare room for this kid."

A sigh. "Yes, Philippe."

Adam heard the woman leave and took the opportunity to remind the man about the blindfold. "You can take it off now," he said. "I assure you it's not necessary. I haven't the slightest idea where we are or how we got here."

All he got in reply was a grunt.

When the woman came back, she said the room would be ready in a few minutes.

"That's a good girl," the man said. "Don't look so worried; I know exactly what I'm doing. Give us a kiss, then."

The woman laughed. "Later, when we're alone. I hope you're going to stay longer this time."

The man sniffed. "Something smells good. I've been so busy looking after business, I haven't eaten since breakfast."

"It's just chili. There's plenty, if you want some."

Adam heard the screech of a chair being pulled out. "Okay, serve it up," the man said. "And lock this kid in the room. He's getting on my nerves, bleating about the blindfold."

"I don't like it, Philippe. How long's he going to be here?"

"Tell you later. I can't talk with my mouth full."

At that, Adam felt the woman's hand on his arm and he was led away.

———

As soon as he heard the woman shut the door and the key turn in the lock, Adam tried to remove the blindfold. It was like a vise, giving him a throbbing headache, but the knot was awkward to get at and too tight to budge. All he managed to do was break a fingernail.

Giving up, he sat down on the bare floor to try and determine why he had been brought here. All he did was trip the chauffeur, who was after Scott. He was completely in the dark. What did they plan to do with him? It was a puzzle.

But a puzzle, in Adam's mind, represented a challenge waiting to be solved, and his brain went to work on it.

All he knew was that the men were after Scott. When he, on the spur of the moment, had stuck out his foot and tripped Scott's pursuer, he was grabbed from behind and dragged into the car, then brought here and locked up. It was as if he was some kind of substitute for Scott, who had gotten away.

Yes, that's what he must represent, a substitute for Scott, like that awful-tasting substitute for coffee in wartime. But who were these guys and why were they after his friend? He and Scott were pretty close; they had no secrets. But they had been working at their separate jobs all day – Adam as a waiter, Scott as a deckhand. Something must have happened – something between Scott and the owner of the Packard or his chauffeur – and Scott hadn't had a chance to tell him about it. Whatever it was, it must be serious for them to go to this extreme.

He sighed and leaned against the wall. When he felt something pressing against his lower back, he remembered he still had his book in his pocket. A sudden urge to get it out and bury his nose in it took hold, to take his mind off his bleak situation. If only he could get the blindfold off! He tried again, but all he managed to do was break another fingernail.

Adam's boredom threshold had always been low. Back home, he was either reading a science book or talking about what he'd been reading. But now he was blindfolded and alone, so he couldn't do either. He got up and made a tour of the room, starting at the door. He felt his way around the walls, expecting at any minute to bump into a bed or bark his shin on a chair. He encountered nothing, not even a window. The room was as bad as an isolation cell in a federal prison.

The rattle of a key in the lock startled him. He heard the door open.

"Who's there?"

«*C'est moi,*» a voice said.

It was a younger voice than that of the woman who'd brought him to the room. A nice voice. "You must be the one they call Colette."

«*Oui. Et vous?*»

"I'm Adam."

"Well, Ad*am,*" she said, switching to English, "I brought you something to eat."

"Smells wonderful. Take off my blindfold, Colette."

"Oh, so you're giving orders now."

"Sorry. Take off my blindfold, *s'il vous plaît.*"

"That's better. And in French, too. Well, I suppose . . . it would be hard to eat blindfolded, and he didn't say not to."

The touch of her hands was gentle and sure. Her soft sweet smell mingled with the spicy aroma of the chili as she worked on the knot behind his head. "Oh, it's so tight. There, now it's coming."

He felt an immense relief and a surge of blood to his head as the blindfold slipped off. «*Ah! Merci beaucoup.*»

The overhead light, a bare bulb, almost blinded him. He squinted up at her through his eyelashes. This made her appear to be shimmering, as if she were an apparition or vision.

As his sight cleared, he saw that she was indeed a vision – a vision of beauty. Adam, with his limited experience with girls, was dumbstruck.

"Hello," she said, as he continued to stare at her.

"Hello," he managed to croak.

She turned to go. «*Et bien! Bon appétit!*»

"Wait, please don't go."

"But if I don't, he'll be in here, wanting to know what's holding me up."

"Come back later then."

"Perhaps. I'll see." She went out, locking the door behind her.

Reluctantly, Adam watched her go, the tray beside him. He gave a long sigh, then took out his book and began to read while he ate.

EIGHT

Adam's hopes of seeing Colette again that night were dashed. The older woman, who he assumed was her mother, came instead. She left two blankets and a pillow for him and took away the tray with the empty dishes. Avoiding his eyes, she didn't say a word.

She also left a pail, which, Adam realized, must be for his toilet. But someone would have to empty it after he used it. How embarrassing, especially if it was Colette!

He spread his blanket and lay down to read more of his book. It was a classic called *Two Years before the Mast,* which he'd bought from a used-book store, thinking he could learn all about being a sailor.

But he'd been teased mercilessly by the old hands when they saw what he was reading. "You won't find many masts to climb around here," Bert, the helmsman, said with a grin, "and the captain put away his cat-o'-nine-tails a few years ago."

Adam was tempted to say, "Yes, but he's still got his temper to whip you with," but restrained himself. He found the book interesting, even if no one else did. Written by a student who dropped out of Harvard in 1834 to sign on as a seaman on the brig *Pilgrim*, it described his two-year voyage around the Horn of South America to California and the hardships the crew had to endure.

Now, exhausted from his long harrowing day, Adam fell asleep on the hard floor. He'd been in the middle of a chapter in which the captain flogs one of the crew and dreamt that the *Rapids Prince* was captured by pirates. He was forced to walk the plank and plunge into the maelstrom, where he was battered by rocks.

Adam woke up sore and stiff from sleeping on the floor. He thought it must be morning, but, as the room had no windows, there was no way to tell. He got up, stretched his aching muscles, and used the bucket. He wished he had something to cover it with – maybe they would let him empty it himself to avoid embarrassment.

Listening at the door, he could hear activity in the

house: footsteps, the murmur of voices – mostly women's but occasionally a man's – doors opening and closing. He was hungry and thirsty. Just as he was wondering if he would get any breakfast, the door opened and Colette came in. She was carrying a tray with a plate of scrambled eggs and toast and a glass of juice.

«*Bonjour, Colette.*»

«*Bonjour,*» she said. "Your breakfast, Adam." He liked the way she said his name, with the stress on the last syllable.

«*Merci beaucoup,*» he responded as he took the tray from her. "It looks delicious." As he tried to get up the nerve to ask if he could empty the slop pail some-where, she seized it by the handle and took it away. Soon, she brought it back empty, so that was that. Not as embarrassing as he'd feared. But then she went to the door again.

"Why do you always rush away, Colette?" he said. "Stay and talk to me."

She stopped, her hand on the doorknob. "Because *maman* is afraid you will attack me and escape," she said. She smiled when she said it, however.

"Attack you? Never."

"I know. But she is nervous about having you here."

"Are you? Nervous, I mean."

She looked at him. "Of course not," she said,

coming over and picking up his book. "Do you like this?"

Adam nodded. "The author was a student who dropped out of Harvard to sign on as a deckhand on the brig –"

"The brig *Pilgrim*," Colette said. "I know. There is a French version."

Adam blinked. "You've read it?"

"I've read all the classics. All I can . . . how do you say it? . . . get my hands on. You, too?"

"Well, I've read *some* classics." Adam couldn't actually recall any classics he'd read except for Shakespeare's *Macbeth* and *Henry V,* both of which had been assigned in school. "I read mostly science books. Anything to do with mathematics, especially. I like math because it's so orderly and universal, if you know what I mean."

Colette nodded. "I know," she said, "like Newton's *Principia Mathematica*." She stopped. "But why are you looking at me like that, Adam?"

Adam realized he'd been staring. She'd read Newton's *Principia Mathematica!* He'd never met anyone like Colette before, never even dreamt that there were girls like her. "Sorry, it's just that . . . just that . . . I didn't expect –"

"Colette!" It was her mother's voice, calling from the hall.

"I must go," she said.

"But why?"

"He told me to deliver the tray and leave. He doesn't trust me."

"Colette!" called her mother again, just outside the door now.

"You mean the man in the gray suit – the one your mother called Philippe?"

"That's him. Philippe Vandam. He orders her around. Me, too, if he can."

"With a car like that he must be rich. What does he do?"

"Who knows. Something mysterious he never talks about."

Her mother pounded on the door. "Colette, what are you doing in there?"

"Coming, *maman*!" She went to the door.

"Come back soon," Adam said. "I beg you on bended knee."

Colette laughed. "You're funny, Adam." Then she left, shutting the door gently behind her.

He stared at the door in such a daze, he forgot about his desperate situation. As long as Colette was around, it didn't seem so bad.

The sounds Adam had been hearing in the house gradually died away. *Perhaps they have all gone out,* he thought. He tried the door, just in case, but it was firmly locked. Colette might be friendly, but she was still his jailer.

Then, when he least expected it, she came in again and leaned against the door, frowning. *She's beautiful even when she frowns,* Adam thought.

"It's very quiet in the house," he said. "I thought you had all left."

"*Maman* has gone to the patisserie. And Mr. Vandam had to go somewhere. I'm glad when he goes away I don't like how he treats *maman* and me, as if we are his servants."

"Will he be back?"

"Oh, yes." She paused. "*Adam?*"

"Yes? What is it, Colette?"

"There is something you should know. He is a dangerous man."

"I've already guessed that."

"But you don't know what he is going to do with you."

Adam felt a jolt of alarm. "No, I don't. Do you?"

She nodded. "I heard him on the telephone. He's having a meeting with others like him. But in another place, not in Montreal."

Adam shrugged. "Well, there's no law against having a meeting. There's not much you or I can do about that. Best we stay out of it, Colette. If he catches you listening to his phone calls –"

"But *you* can't stay out of it, Ad*am*," Colette interrupted. "That's why I am telling you. *Maman* won't let Mr. Vandam leave you here when he goes away, and he said he won't free you."

"*Uh-oh*. What's he going to do with me then?"

"He's taking you with him."

Adam started. "Good God. Where?"

"I didn't hear where. But he said he is going to meet with the others at an inn on the river. Something secret to do with the war, but he will say they are there for a fishing trip."

Just then a door slammed. "Oh!" Colette said. "*Maman*'s back already. I can't let her find me here." She slipped out and quietly turned the key, leaving a worried Adam behind.

NINE

The night before, following the directions from the man on the steps, Scott had come to a main intersection and turned left. Sure enough, it wasn't long before he saw the outline of the *Rapids Prince* at the end of the street. The ship was still tied up at the pier, as if it had been patiently waiting for him all this time.

Victoria Pier itself was empty, however. The taxis, buses, and tourists had all left. He'd expected that Lindsay, at least, would still be there, with her father and mother. He had, in fact, worried about them pacing the pier, distraught over his and Adam's fate and waiting anxiously for them to return.

But when Scott saw that there was no one waiting, either on the pier or on the deck of the *Rapids Prince*, he was taken aback. They would have been appalled at his foolishness – leaping onto the bumper of a speeding car – and wouldn't have had any idea why he did it.

In a way, it was a relief that he didn't have to face them right now. For if he did, he would have to lie to them about Adam's whereabouts. Not lie exactly, but not tell all that he knew. Not so much a sin of commission as of omission, as the minister back home was fond of saying.

It would be a hard part for him to play. Especially with Lindsay, who often seemed to know exactly what he was thinking. And with the police too, if they became involved. But for Adam's sake, he would have to do it.

As Scott approached the ship, there was still no sign of anyone. He'd thought *someone* would be anxious for word about Adam, if not about him. Maybe no one saw Adam being hauled into the backseat of the Packard. Certainly no one had any idea that the men who'd taken him were German agents. No one except him.

Come to think of it, not even Adam knew. And Scott knew only because of his interest in the Packard Twelve Touring Sedan that was parked on the pier in Prescott that morning. Yet his hands were tied; he couldn't say anything about what he'd heard without endangering Adam's life. It was just as well no one was here to meet him.

Suddenly, he was utterly exhausted. It had been a

long day. All he wanted to do was flop into his bunk and sleep. He trudged up the gangway.

As he did, a dim figure appeared from the shadows, where it had been keeping watch. "Scott!" the figure cried. "It's really you at last!"

He looked up. Lindsay rushed to him and threw her arms around him. He felt her tears on his neck.

"We've been calling all the hospitals, expecting to hear you'd been in a terrible accident. Are you all right?"

"Of course. I'm fine." He hugged her tightly, feeling the energy flow back into him. "I'm sorry I worried you, jumping on the bumper like that. I wasn't thinking."

"Everyone thought you were crazy, but I knew you must have had a reason. And Adam? Where is Adam? He's disappeared too."

"I-I'm not sure."

Lindsay pulled back and looked at him questioningly. "What do you mean, you're not sure? Is he all right?"

She knows I'm holding out, he thought. *She as good as reads my mind.*

"Something's happened to Adam, hasn't it?" she said.

He made a sudden decision. He'd tell her, the one person he trusted completely, but only her. He looked around nervously. "I have to be careful," he said. "If I give him away, he'll take it out on Adam."

She frowned. "Who will?"

"The man who grabbed him."

"What man? Scott, what are you saying?"

He heaved a sigh. "It's a long story. I overheard something I wasn't supposed to hear. I'll tell you, but nobody else. For Adam's sake."

He led her to the bench and sat down beside her. "It began this morning, when we were still at the pier in Prescott. . . ."

"So you see why I mustn't tell anyone," he said, when he finished. "Not even your mother and father – or Adam's parents."

"Oh, Scott, that will be terribly hard. And poor Adam. His family will be so worried. You've got to tell them *something*. What are you going to say?"

Scott studied a bare patch on the deck where the strong soda solution they scrubbed with had wrinkled the surface. The frown lines on his forehead deepened. "I've been thinking and thinking about it while I was finding my way back here. I guess all I can say is that I fell off and never saw where the Packard ended up. I hate lying, but –"

"They'll ask more than that, though, Scott. And if

they call in the police, they'll want to know why Adam was taken."

Scott shrugged. "I know. I can only pretend I don't know anything."

"Scott, that's not good enough."

"Don't I know it! My only hope is that they release Adam soon." He looked around at the empty deck. "But where is everybody?"

"Mom and Dad are in the purser's office, phoning every place they can think of – the hospitals, the police. We'd better let them know you're back. They'll be awfully relieved."

Lindsay kept a firm grip on Scott's hand as they crossed the deck, as if determined never to lose him again.

TEN

Adam paced the room restlessly. The man in the gray suit – Vandam, Colette called him – was going away. To some kind of secret meeting disguised as a fishing trip. But the really disturbing news was that Vandam planned to keep him a prisoner and take him along.

But why? he wondered. If Colette's mother wouldn't let Vandam leave him here any longer, why didn't he just let him go? Hauling him to some meeting, and keeping him locked up, would be a lot of trouble. There could be only one reason to go to all that bother – whatever Scott had learned about him must be something highly secretive. Only by keeping him hostage could Vandam be sure Scott wouldn't talk.

But what could it possibly be?

Adam felt like he'd been transported to some surreal

world, where nothing made sense. At the same time, it reminded him of something, but he couldn't think quite what. Something Scott had said recently . . .

The door opened and Colette slipped in. She had paper and a pen in her hand. "I thought you'd want to send a message to someone before you leave," she said. "To let them know you're all right. I can take it to the post office if you want."

"That's very brave of you, but it's risky," Adam said. "What if Vandam or your mother finds out?"

"I will take that chance. *Maman* cares for him, but she cares for me more."

Adam looked at her, concerned. "Are you sure you want to do this? You said he's dangerous."

"Let me worry about that," Colette said. "You just write the note."

For the first time, he saw how strong-willed she could be. "All right," he said. "I'll just say I'm well, with some people I met, and not to worry. I don't dare tell them I'm being held captive, or they will rush right down to the police. And if Vandam finds out the police are on his trail, I could end up in the river, with my feet encased in cement!" He shuddered. "And, if they *do* catch up to Vandam, they could charge all three of you with kidnapping and forcible confinement, even though it's all Vandam's doing. I know it sounds crazy, but trust me – it's for the best."

Colette sighed. "I suppose. But I have to go now. I'll come back later for the letter."

While Adam was composing the note to his parents, he became aware of loud voices in the house. It sounded like an argument. He finished his letter and sat waiting for Colette.

It wasn't until lunchtime that she appeared, carrying a tray with a sandwich and a glass of milk. He gave her the letter, and she slipped it in her pocket. "I heard people arguing," he said. "Is there trouble?"

"It was *maman* and Vandam. She doesn't want me to go."

"Go where?"

"With the rest of you."

"You're coming too? Wonderful!"

She nodded. "He wants me to look after the farmhouse he's rented, where you will be locked up. The chauffeur and another man will guard you. It's near the inn where Vandam and the others will be. That's what the argument was all about. 'I don't want Colette there with those men,' Mama said.

"But Vandam said no one would dare bother me and he'd pay me well to do the cooking. I'd make a lot more money than at my part-time library job, he said. They argued, but he won. He always wins. 'It's a nice place, right on the St. Lawrence,' he said. 'It'll be like a paid summer holiday for Colette.' But *maman* replied, 'Some holiday looking after those men!'"

"So the chauffeur will be in the farmhouse with you and me and the other man, too," Adam said. "Maybe he's the one I saw in the car before. Who is he anyway?"

"All I know is, he's called Heinrik sometimes, Howard other times," Colette said. "These different names they use are confusing."

"That's their purpose," Adam said. "To confuse people. Howard is probably an alias."

"Ah, I see." Colette went to the door. "I'll go and mail your letter now. I guess we'll all be in the same car tomorrow. But we'd better not act too friendly, Adam," she warned. "Vandam might get suspicious."

As the door closed behind Colette, Adam felt lost. *But at least she'll continue to bring me my meals at the farmhouse,* he thought.

That night, as he tried to get to sleep, he lay wondering where, exactly, they'd be going. A farmhouse near an inn on the St. Lawrence, Colette had said. From what he'd seen from the deck of the *Rapids Prince,* there weren't that many inns right on the water. There was, however, one near Prescott, where Lindsay had a summer job. *I couldn't be that lucky, could I?*

———

On Tuesday morning, Vandam entered the room and blindfolded him again.

"Must you?" Adam said, but Vandam didn't bother answering. Instead, he yanked him roughly along the hall and down the outside stairs, a blindfolded Adam stumbling behind.

He'd hoped that he'd be seated close to Colette, but Vandam shoved him in the front seat beside Twitch and climbed in the back with her and the man called Heinrik.

For a while, Adam heard nothing but the purring of the Packard's engine. Eventually he began to hear other cars as traffic increased around them.

The speaking-tube squawked and he heard Vandam say, "Better stop here and take off his blindfold, Twitch. People are starting to notice. Don't let him try any funny business, like signaling other cars."

Twitch pulled over to the curb, and Adam felt fingers fumbling with the knot. Then the blindfold slid off. "You heard Mr. Vandam," Twitch said gruffly. "No funny business." He opened his chauffeur's jacket and showed a blackjack tucked in his belt. "Don't make me use this. Not that I'd mind belting you one, if I had to."

"Don't worry, Twitch," Adam said. "I'll just sit here

nice and quiet. Shall I get out the map and help you navigate?" He reached for the glove compartment.

Twitch swatted his arm down. "Leave it! And don't call me Twitch. My name's Tyler to you."

Adam lapsed into a temporary silence. *Better not push him too far.* Anyway, it was a nice change from the room, having a cushy seat to sit on.

He glanced in the back. The man called Heinrik was on the backseat with Vandam, a muzzled German shepherd sprawled on the floor in front of them. Colette, he saw, was on the jump seat, engrossed in a book. He almost smiled at her before he remembered her warning not to act friendly.

Vandam noticed him looking back and scowled. Adam sighed and returned to watch the scenery.

As they left Montreal, the landscape changed from city streets with wall-to-wall buildings to farmland, where cows paused in their grazing to stare at them. The occasional church steeple loomed on the horizon to announce the presence of a town ahead.

The winding two-lane highway was identified by signs as the KING'S HIGHWAY 2. At intervals, the signs would say CORNWALL 70 MILES or TORONTO 310 MILES, so Adam knew they were headed west.

The highway took them alongside a lengthy strip

of canal, which looked vaguely familiar to him. It was, he realized suddenly, the Soulanges Canal, looking much different when viewed from the highway than from the deck of the *Rapids Prince*. Watching a freighter in one of the locks, he remembered, with a shudder, how he'd stumbled around there in the middle of the night, hauling in the *Rapids Prince's* heavy lines when he was still a deckhand.

Vandam's voice came over the speaking-tube. "Go slow along here, Twitch," he ordered.

Adam snuck another look back. Both Vandam and Heinrik were staring at the canal, talking in low voices. He saw that Heinrik was making notes, and he wished he could hear what they were saying. In the jump seat, Colette appeared to be buried in her book.

He couldn't know that she was actually paying close attention to what the two men behind her were saying. She wasn't sure what she'd gotten herself into on this trip, and she was determined to find out more. They kept their voices so low that she had trouble following. But she did hear Heinrik say something about explosives. And that troubled her.

Eventually, the road veered away from the canal, and they entered the town of Cornwall. Then Adam knew exactly where they were and that they would come to Prescott, the home port for the *Rapids Prince,* if they kept going.

When they reached Prescott, he looked for the smokestack of the *Rapids Prince,* but the highway did not go close enough to the waterfront. Though it seemed a long time since that fateful night at Victoria Pier, it had been only two nights ago.

He had a sudden burst of affection for Scott and his other shipmates, and he ached to be out of this mess and back on board. Even Captain Plum would be a welcome sight! But he'd better not think about that anymore, he decided. If he wasn't careful, he'd start feeling sorry for himself. At least he was back on familiar ground.

They continued on through Prescott and took the highway out of town. Then Vandam told Twitch to slow down as the turnoff was just ahead.

Twitch made a left turn onto the dirt road that was marked by a sign that read THE BLINKBONNIE INN, COTTAGES, GUEST ROOMS, MEETING ROOMS & FINE DINING, ONE MILE.

Adam had to hide his elation. The Blinkbonnie – that *was* the inn where Lindsay said she had a summer job! *Is it just coincidence that Vandam will be holding his meeting at an inn close to the town where the* Rapids Prince *docks? Is there some reason he and his associates want to be near the ship?*

As the car headed down the dirt road towards the river, it hit a bump and scraped bottom. The low-slung Packard might be smooth on highways, but it wasn't made for country roads. Twitch swore and slammed on the brakes.

Through the trees, the river sparkled, as if luring them on despite the rough road. Everyone hung on as the car bounced over the bumps. When they reached the Blinkbonnie, the car turned in, pulled up to the front door, and stopped.

Yes! Adam said to himself triumphantly. There was hope yet, with Lindsay so close. And where Lindsay was, Scott wouldn't be far behind.

The Blinkbonnie turned out to be a sprawling two-story log building, with a colorful awning over the entrance. The *plonk* of balls sounded from the tennis courts, and the buzz of outboard motors drifted up from the river.

A bellhop came smartly up to the car, and Twitch got out and opened the trunk. "Mr. Dale's party checking in," he said, remembering Vandam's instructions.

The moment Twitch got out, Adam seized the chance he'd been waiting for. Pulling his novel out of his back pocket, he tore out several pages and crumpled them up. As Vandam headed inside to register, followed by Twitch, he unobtrusively dropped one out the window.

He watched it bounce off the running board and fall onto the road. *Maybe, just maybe, Lindsay or Scott will notice it and realize who must have dropped it. It's worth a try!*

ELEVEN

Lindsay was on the desk when the elegantly dressed man and his chauffeur came in. She looked at the registration card he filled out. It took a minute to decipher his scrawl. *G. Phillip Dale*, it read.

"Yes, Mr. Dale. Welcome to the Blinkbonnie. We've reserved rooms for you and your guests, as you requested, and the farmhouse for your staff." She tapped the bell on the counter. "The bellhop will show you to your room."

"Have the others arrived yet?" he asked.

"Not yet, Mr. Dale."

"Then advise me as soon as they do," he said brusquely.

The bellhop reached for his briefcase. "Not that one," Vandam said sharply. "I'll take it. You bring the suitcase." He picked up the briefcase and strode to the elevator as Twitch stepped up to ask about the route to the farmhouse.

"You continue on the same road for a quarter mile," Lindsay explained, "then turn away from the river at the first crossroad. You'll see it on the right-hand side, about half a mile back from the river. It's the only house on the road."

As he left, the chauffeur's head swiveled nervously from the moth-eaten stuffed bear on a stand to the toothy muskellunge and the record-breaking large-mouth bass mounted on the wall, as if they might take a bite out of him.

Lindsay watched him go, puzzled. He looked familiar, but she couldn't figure out where she'd seen him before.

After the Packard left, the bellhop went back outside to greet the next arrivals. Wrinkled from years in the sun, he was one of the few original staff members remaining among the host of summer students working at the inn. His father had always insisted on keeping a clean yard at home, and the practice was ingrained in his son. When he noticed the page Adam had dropped, he automatically picked up the crumpled paper and disposed of it in the refuse bin.

"Litterbugs," he said, shaking his head.

———

In the Packard, Adam had no way of knowing that his signal for Lindsay had been disposed of by the bellhop. He did, however, manage to drop one more crumpled page on the road before the Packard pulled up in front of the isolated two-story farmhouse.

Ordering Adam to stay where he was, Twitch opened the car door for Colette and Heinrik; then he tugged on the German shepherd's leash and coaxed it out. The dog stretched and yawned, as much as it could with its muzzle on, revealing long sharp teeth, then it dragged Twitch over to the nearest tree and relieved itself.

The farmhouse was badly in need of paint, but it had shutters and a covered veranda. Inside the farmhouse, they found linoleum floors, a living room, a big kitchen, and three bedrooms upstairs with one down.

Twitch pointed to the smallest of the three bedrooms upstairs. "Yours," he said to Adam.

Well, at least it has a bed, Adam thought, *and a window.*

"But don't get any ideas," Twitch said. "I'll nail your shutters closed, and your door will be securely locked."

Heinrik let Colette choose from the other two bedrooms, then took his kit bag into the remaining one and closed the door.

"I'm hungry," Adam said. "Anyone for lunch?"

Twitch snorted, shoved him into the small bedroom, and locked the door.

TWELVE

That same evening, Scott and Lindsay strolled hand in hand on the road to the cabins, where Lindsay lived with the other staff working at the Blinkbonnie.

"I'm so glad you're back," she said. "I was worried about you. It must have been a difficult trip from Montreal, with everyone asking you where Adam was."

"It was hard, all right," Scott said, "especially when I had to phone Adam's parents and make all those excuses."

"If only there was some way I could help," Lindsay said.

"Trouble is, it's only going to get worse if Adam isn't freed in the next few days," Scott went on. "Captain Plum keeps after me about him. I don't know how long I can hold off a full-scale search, and you know what that could mean."

He shuddered as he recalled Vandam's warning. *Would he really carry out his threat?* He hoped he never had to find out.

The day after the fatal Sunday excursion, the *Rapids Prince* had made its usual return trip from Montreal through the canal and was now docked at Prescott, preparing for the next trip down the rapids. Scott had hardly been able to wait for work to finish so he could make his way to the inn to see Lindsay. On Tuesday, he'd hitched a ride west along the highway to the turnoff and walked down the road to the Blinkbonnie.

Now, as they made their way to her cabin, Lindsay stooped to pick up a crumpled piece of paper from the road. "I try to keep this place looking neat," she said, "but it's a losing battle."

Scott stared at the paper. It looked like a page from a book.

"What, Scott?"

"Let me see that. But how could . . . no, I can't believe it. . . ."

"What? Tell me!"

"That paper. It's a page from the same book Adam carries everywhere with him on the ship. See, the title's at the top – *Two Years before the Mast*. But Adam is in Montreal; it can't be from his book."

"If only he *was* here," Lindsay said. She stopped

suddenly and put her hand to her mouth. "Oh, that's who that man is! Of course!"

"What man?"

"The chauffeur who wanted directions to the farmhouse. I thought he looked familiar. He's the same one I saw at Victoria Pier. You were talking to me, and he came over to ask if you wanted to look at the Packard now. Remember?"

Scott stared at her in astonishment. "The chauffeur from the Packard? He's here? Are you sure?"

"It's him, I know it. He's staying at the farmhouse. And the man he works for is at the inn. He registered as G. Phillip Dale."

Scott was so excited, he couldn't contain himself. He grabbed Lindsay's arm. "It's Vandam! Does that mean Adam's here too? Is this crumpled page a signal from him? It must be! He knew you worked here. This is just the sort of thing Adam would do."

"And now he's being held in the farmhouse, I'll bet," Lindsay said, "where the chauffeur is staying . . . but what can we do about it? We don't dare tell anyone."

Scott's excitement was slowly ebbing away. "You're right. Even if he is here, we're in the same old bind."

Anything they thought of doing carried the same risk to Adam's life. *A rescue attempt? Going to the police? Surrounding the farmhouse?* "There's nothing we can do," Scott finally said.

"I know. It's so frustrating." They walked on in a gloomy silence.

"But maybe there *is* something we can do!" Lindsay said suddenly.

Scott stopped in his tracks. "Like what?"

"You could turn the tables on this Vandam," Lindsay replied.

"How do you mean?"

"Well, he's a spy, isn't he?"

Scott nodded.

"So *you* spy on *him*. Uncover his secrets. You might find out if Adam is in the farmhouse too. You might even discover which room he's in."

"I'd like nothing better," Scott said, "but I can't go wandering around the inn without someone stopping me, wanting to know what I'm doing there."

"You could if you were a bellhop," Lindsay said.

"Yes, but I'm not. I'm a deckhand who's due for work in the morning."

"Which means you've most of the night," Lindsay said. "And there's a spare bellhop's uniform in the clean laundry that came back this morning."

"Hey, great idea!" Scott said. "But, Lindsay, if your boss finds out, you could lose your job."

"So? Adam could lose his life. That's a lot more important. I'll take the chance."

———

Scott tried to act like he belonged at the inn, but felt uncomfortable in the tight-fitting uniform – he'd had to yank hard on the smart blue jacket to close it enough for the buttons to reach, and the collar was so tight it was choking him. But it would have to do.

He adjusted his pillbox cap, like the bellhop in the commercial who intoned *Call for Philip Morris*, and continued along the upstairs hall, looking for room number 226. Vandam had already gone in to dinner, Lindsay had told him, so this was his chance.

Room 222, 224, ah, there it is. Scott glanced around to make sure the hallway was empty, then took out the passkey she'd given him.

Once inside the room, he looked for Vandam's briefcase, but all he could see was a suitcase on the luggage stand. It took him precious minutes to find the briefcase, which was concealed behind some clothes and a folding card table in the closet. He hauled it out, but its gold clasp was securely locked.

The rattle of the doorknob startled him. He hurriedly shoved the briefcase back in the closet as the door was flung open.

Vandam strode in. He stopped short when he saw Scott. "Hey, what are you doing in my room?"

Scott froze. Keeping his back to Vandam, he tried desperately to think of an excuse for being there.

"*Ah,* there he is," a voice called from the doorway.

"Who?" Vandam said. Glancing around, Scott saw him jerk his thumb in Scott's direction. "You mean him?"

The red-haired man at the door nodded. "I've been waiting for a bellhop. He was supposed to come and pick up my suit for pressing."

"Dumb kid," Vandam said. "I wondered what he was up to in my closet."

Totally bewildered by this unexpected turn of events, Scott took advantage of the opportunity to head for the door, keeping his face averted as he passed Vandam. He didn't dare look at him, remembering that Vandam had seen him up close as he was trying to escape from the back of the Packard on Sunday. He prayed he wouldn't recognize him in the bellhop's uniform.

"I'm awfully sorry, sir," he mumbled. "I thought the desk clerk said room 226. I was looking for the suit in your closet. My mistake."

"Oh, just get out of here," Vandam growled, and slammed the door behind him.

Relieved, but still very much at sea, Scott turned to ask his savior's room number. *What a lucky coincidence,* he thought. *The man has a suit to be pressed at just the right time!*

But the hallway was empty. The red-haired man had mysteriously disappeared. *Is it really a coincidence that he claimed to have a suit for pressing, or is something else going on?*

"Who do you suppose he was?" Scott asked Lindsay when he was back at the front desk. "He said he asked for a suit to be picked up, but then he vanished."

"It's so puzzling," Lindsay said. "What did he look like?"

"Tall, red-haired . . ."

"There was a red-haired man who checked in this morning – one of Vandam's associates," Lindsay said. "But no one called for a suit to be picked up."

"It's an enigma. But he sure saved my bacon," Scott said, still shaky from his close call. "So what do we do now? I don't dare risk trying Vandam's room again."

"He's reserved a conference room for tonight," Lindsay said. "You could eavesdrop on their meeting, if you're up to it. You still look pale; maybe you've done enough for tonight."

But Scott knew there was no stopping now. "I'll be all right in a minute. Where is this place they're meeting?"

"Just down the hall. We could have a look at it when my shift is over. Better stay in here for now." She opened the door to a storage room behind the desk.

Scott went in, unbuttoned his vest, and settled down on a pile of laundry to wait. So far he'd been lucky. Saved by the timely appearance of the red-haired man, he hadn't run into the bellhop on duty, who Lindsay had gotten out of the way by sending him to sort out the luggage room. He'd also managed to avoid the other staff members – except for one of the maids, who had given him a funny look on his way to Vandam's room.

But would his luck hold? It looked like it was going to be a long night. . . .

The next thing Scott knew, someone was shaking him by the shoulder. He opened his eyes.

Lindsay was leaning over him. "Time to go," she whispered. "Better change into your street clothes – the bellhop on duty is back. I'll rap on the door when the coast is clear."

Scott put on his clothes, glad to get out of the tight-fitting uniform. When he heard a rap on the door, he opened it cautiously. There was no one around, except an elderly couple in the lobby studying a map.

"Go down the hall to conference room 111," Lindsay whispered. "It's open. I'll meet you there in ten minutes."

When Scott found room 111, he slipped inside and

felt for the light switch, then changed his mind. Someone from the staff might look in and see him.

He explored the room for possibilities, as much as he could in the dark. It was small, as conference rooms go, with a dozen chairs around a circular table. A raised platform at the far end was framed by curtains.

The door opened and a figure was silhouetted in the doorway. Scott tensed as a hand reached in and clicked the light switch. *Phew, it's Lindsay.*

"Glad you're here," he said. "I'm wondering where to hide. Any suggestions?"

"They won't be using the stage," Lindsay said. "Let's have a look."

At the back of the stage, they found a storage cupboard containing a screen and projector. "Perfect," Scott said. "I can listen from behind the curtain, but I can duck into the cupboard if I have to."

Lindsay looked doubtful. "Risky. If they find you, you're trapped. Maybe this isn't such a good idea."

"But we've got to do something before it's too late," Scott insisted.

"I suppose," Lindsay said reluctantly. "Their meeting's scheduled for seven. How late can you stay?"

He shrugged. "All night if I have to. As long as I'm back in time for work in the morning."

"I'll leave you then." She gave him a hug. "Come

to my cabin when the meeting's over. Good luck!"

He held on to her until she slipped out of his arms and walked away.

Then he arranged the curtains so there was a small gap, just enough to peer through without being seen, and he sat down to wait.

As soon as Scott heard the door open, he risked a peek through the crack in the curtains and saw it was Vandam. Beside him was the blond man called Heinrik, who Scott had glimpsed in the Packard the night of his wild ride through the streets of Montreal.

A moment later another man arrived, then several more. Vandam introduced Heinrik, and, greeting him warmly, they congratulated him on his successful landing from the U-boat.

When the last person arrived, Vandam said, "Now that we're all here, let's get started."

Scott heard the click of a lock. He saw Vandam opening his briefcase and taking out a map.

"Our target is shown in detail here," Vandam said, spreading out the map on the table. "Heinrik will, of course, be the one planting the device, but each of us has a part to play in backing him up. The code name for the mission is Operation Blockade." The others gathered around the map, murmuring their approval.

Scott groaned inwardly. If only he could have gotten into that briefcase, he would have seen what their target was.

"Our subs are already playing havoc with the enemy's Atlantic lifeline," Vandam said. "Operation Blockade will add to their valiant work and help shorten the war. *Herr Hitler* will reward us." There was applause.

"In the meantime," he said, "Walther, here, has arranged for a boat. This is supposed to be a fishing trip. But, in reality, he'll be using the boat to explore the American side of the river. We'll be ready to cross the border, under cover of darkness, when this operation is over. Then we will continue our work in the United States."

The men sat around the table for some time, discussing each person's role. Vandam stressed the importance of absolute secrecy. "Anyone we suspect of being a risk to our operation will be eliminated," he said.

To Scott, it was one more reminder of the ruthlessness of these people. What did he think he was playing at? This was no game! And yet, there was no other way. Either that, or leave Adam to his fate.

"One more caution," Vandam warned. "If, at any time, this operation is compromised, it will be abandoned immediately. Other projects are equally important, and we must, at all costs, avoid detection. That is all for tonight. We'll meet again tomorrow."

He raised his right arm, and Scott thought for a moment he was going to say *Heil Hitler*, but Vandam was too cautious for that. The others raised their right arms in response and then began to file out.

Well, that's that, Scott thought. He hadn't learned anything to help him rescue Adam, but he *had* learned that they were planning something called Operation Blockade to disrupt Allied shipping.

It was time to go. As he crossed the stage, a board creaked under him.

"What was that?" a voice said.

Scott froze.

THIRTEEN

With pounding heart, Scott waited. Then he heard Vandam say, "I'd better check. We can't be too careful." He dove into the cupboard.

"No, you stay here," someone else said. "I'll go."

Footsteps crossed the stage. Scott closed his eyes as the cupboard door was yanked open.

After a moment of silence, the cupboard door was closed. He heard the footsteps recross the stage. *Is he going for reinforcements?* Scott wondered.

"Must have been the wind," the man said. "It's getting stronger; I think we're in for a blow."

The next thing Scott knew, the lights went out and the conference-room door slammed shut. He began to breathe again.

How lucky can you get? Twice he'd come within a hair of being caught, only to be saved. *Was it by the same man?* He was still as jumpy as a cat chasing leaves in the wind as he slipped out the side door of the inn. Taking the path through the woods, he headed for Lindsay's cabin.

An east wind was moaning in the treetops. In this part of the world, it usually meant stormy weather for three days. The dark shapes of elms lined the path on both sides. Suddenly, a figure stepped out from behind a tree and blocked his way.

Scott jumped.

"What the heck are you up to, son?" the figure said. "That's the second time."

The second time? Scott peered through the gloom. It was the man with the red hair who'd saved him in Vandam's room. It must have been him in the conference room, too, Scott realized.

"I don't know how to thank you for coming to my rescue," Scott said. "Lucky for me you were there, or –"

"Never mind that. Who are you, anyway?"

"I'm Scott. Scott Graves."

"I don't mean your name. What were you doing back there, and how did you get mixed up with Vandam and his gang?"

Scott made a quick decision that this was a man he

could trust – he'd saved him twice. "Well, you see, sir, it was like this: I have a job as a deckhand on the *Rapids Prince,* and Mr. Vandam was on board last Sunday and –"

"You mean you were on the *Rapids Prince* when my colleague Derek Patterson went overboard?"

"Derek Patterson was your colleague?"

"Derek Patterson is . . . I mean was . . . the one who'd been following Heinrik since he landed from the U-boat. We weren't ready to nab Heinrik yet as we wanted to see who his contacts were first."

"But who *was* Derek Patterson? And who are you?"

The man sighed. "I guess I need to explain. I'm from the FBI –"

"The FBI!"

"And Derek Patterson was with the Canadian security services," the man went on. "We're working together. Unfortunately for Derek, they caught on to him before we were ready to move in. I've managed to infiltrate Vandam's gang, but they'll eliminate me too if they find out who I am. This is wartime, and it's a dangerous game we're playing. A kid like you shouldn't get involved. And I can't save you every time, or they'll begin to suspect me."

"But I *can't* stop now," Scott protested. "Vandam is holding my friend Adam hostage, so I can't tell anyone what I know or he'll take it out on him. I was hoping to find out for sure if Adam's at the farmhouse. Maybe you can help me."

The red-haired man shook his head. "I've helped you all I can. My orders are to stay with the gang until we find out who's behind their operation, both here and in the United States. Then we'll nab the bunch of them."

"But they're planning something here first!" Scott exclaimed. "This Operation Blockade, you've got to stop it or –"

"Don't worry, we're keeping our options open," the man said. "But Vandam could easily change his mind, if he gets nervous about this project, and cross the border for their next mission. In that case –" A branch creaked and the man looked around, startled.

"Look, son, I have to get back before Vandam gets suspicious. Maybe they'll let your friend go if you wait them out. And keep your mouth shut about any of this in the meantime. Understand?" He faded back into the woods.

Scott stood there, hearing only the moaning of the wind. It seemed to surround him, taunting his inability to help Adam.

At the cabin, Scott found Lindsay waiting anxiously. He told her about the man who had, again, got him out of a tight corner. When he mentioned that the man was with the FBI, she became even more anxious. "The FBI! Maybe you should take his advice."

"But his advice was to wait them out. I can't do that or Adam's parents or the police or *someone* will organize a search and . . . well, you know what will happen to Adam then." He pictured Vandam drawing his hand across his throat. "On top of everything else, I found out at their meeting that they have a target somewhere around here. I won't know where unless I can get hold of that map of Vandam's."

"But you can't risk going back to the inn tonight," Lindsay said.

The wind rattled the branches scraping the cabin roof. Scott went to the door and peered out. "Don't worry. I'll just scout out the farmhouse and see if I can figure out which room they have Adam locked up in. It's going to be a wild night, and the storm will cover any noise I make."

"Just be careful," Lindsay said reluctantly.

FOURTEEN

When Adam heard the chauffeur outside his window nailing the shutters closed, each blow of the hammer reminded him that there was no escape.

He hoped Colette hadn't forgotten him. He'd had nothing to eat since breakfast, and it was now early evening.

Finally he heard a key turn in the lock, and in came Colette. "My poor Ad*am,* you must be starving," she said. "I had to order the groceries, then Tyler had to pick them up at the inn."

Adam noticed that Colette was the only one who referred to the chauffeur as Tyler. She thought Twitch was a cruel name.

"Where's Heinrik then?" he said.

"He was here this afternoon, but Vandam called and told him to go over to the inn. They're having some kind of meeting tonight."

He took the tray eagerly. "Smells great. Stay with me while I eat."

"I can't stay. But I did learn something interesting on the trip here. I was listening to Mr. Vandam talking to Heinrik while I pretended to read, and I found out a lot about him. He's not an ordinary businessman like he tells *maman*, he's a Nazi agent."

"A Nazi agent!" Adam said.

"Not only that, but he and Heinrik were studying the canal very carefully as we drove by."

"I saw that," Adam said, "but I couldn't hear a thing they were saying."

"All I heard was the word 'sabotage' and something about an explosion."

"Sabotage! Explosion!"

"Yes, and I don't like it. We should do something about it."

"But what can I do when I'm locked up in here?" Adam said gloomily.

"Nothing while you're their prisoner. But if you were to escape . . ."

Adam sighed. "If only I could. But there's Twitch . . . and Heinrik."

"Heinrik is at the inn," Colette said. "And I can distract Tyler long enough for you get away."

Adam's heart leaped.

Just then, Twitch called up the stairs, "Colette! Where are you?"

"He's waiting for his dinner," Colette said, heading to the door. "I'll tell you more later. Just be ready when I come back."

"But, Colette, they'll blame you!"

She put her finger to her lips, and then she was gone.

Impatient for her return, Adam let his mind race. So Vandam was a Nazi agent, and he and Heinrik were planning sabotage. He remembered now what Scott had said – that there were rumors of a German agent landing in Canada from a submarine. He hadn't taken it seriously at the time, but he did now.

And Colette had an idea to help him escape. *Is she going to distract Twitch by flirting?* French girls were thought to be flirtatious. At least that was what some of the guys said when they heard he was going to be in Montreal this summer. But, no, he couldn't believe Colette would do that. It just wasn't her style. She must have something else in mind.

If Adam did manage to escape, he wondered where he should go from the farmhouse. He could follow the road back to the main highway and try hitching a ride to Prescott and the ship. But as soon as Twitch discovered he was gone, he would, most likely, go after him in the car. So forget the road.

He'd have to stick to the woods. He'd use the woods for cover and head for the lake, then follow the lake to Prescott. Yes, that was the only way. But he was a city boy, and the thought of being alone in the woods at night gave him the jitters. *There are wild animals out there, aren't there?* He had to admit he wasn't the bravest of souls.

Still it had to be done. What mattered was to escape. He just hoped that Colette wouldn't shoulder the blame. He gobbled his dinner, anxious for her return.

When she came back, Colette started talking as soon as she'd shut the door behind her. "I have only a minute, so listen carefully. When I leave with your tray, I won't lock the door."

"But where is Twitch?"

"In the kitchen. I asked him what his favorite dish was and he said *tourtière*. So I said I'd make it for him if he'd grate the carrots and chop the celery for salad. He's doing that now, and it will keep him occupied long enough for you to sneak by and out the back door.

"From there, you're on your own. I wish I could tell you which way to go, but I can't. I can only wish you adieu and God speed, my sweet Adam. I will miss you."

"And I will miss you, Colette," Adam said. "You have been wonderful."

She picked up his tray. "Now I must get back before Tyler wonders what I'm doing."

"Wait. Won't they blame you for my escape?"

"Don't worry about that. I'll say you must have picked the lock. Look after yourself, *mon cher ami Anglais*. Oh, and you'll need this." She handed him a package wrapped in newspaper. "It's for the dog."

Adam blanched. "The guard dog! I forgot about him."

"Give him the steak bone, and he's your friend for life. His name's Pierre," Colette said. Then she opened the door and slipped out. This time there was no click of the lock.

Adam waited long enough for her to get back to the kitchen, then he tiptoed down the stairs. At the bottom, he listened to the murmur of voices and a radio playing low. Taking a deep breath, he snuck past the doorway of the kitchen without looking in, his heart in his mouth. He was half-expecting a shout of alarm any second.

But no shout came. Carefully he opened the back door and stepped out.

He was greeted by a menacing growl.

"Here, Pierre," he whispered, his voice quivering. He opened the package and dropped the bone on the ground, praying that the dog was hungry.

Pierre sniffed at it and then began gnawing at the bone noisily.

Adam backed away, turned, and stumbled into the woods.

FIFTEEN

Scott made his way cautiously along the road in the direction Lindsay said would take him to the farmhouse. It was a dark night, with heavy clouds obscuring the moon and stars. A gust of wind raised a miniature whirlwind of dust around him, and he held his breath until it passed.

Ahead, the lights of the farmhouse appeared, winking through the trees. The house was set back from the road, and the lights from the windows made it look, deceivingly, like a welcome refuge. Sensing a storm coming, he wondered which one of the windows faced the room Adam was held captive in.

Scott could see the shape of a car in the driveway. He kept going until he was close enough to make out the trunk and luggage rack, and the small rear window. He remembered the car well from his precarious ride through Old Montreal. *It's the Packard, all right!*

Suddenly, a ferocious barking broke out behind the farmhouse.

A guard dog! He stayed rooted to the spot, hoping the dog was chained up. A door opened at the back and light spilled out. Someone came outside and spoke to the dog. Then a figure appeared, making a circuit of the house. Scott dove into the ditch beside the driveway and waited until he heard the back door shut again.

He retreated down the road. At least he'd confirmed that the Packard was there and very likely Adam as well. What to do about it was something else again.

Suddenly another volley of barking broke out behind the house. Looking over his shoulder, Scott saw a figure making for the Packard.

The car's lights came on, piercing the darkness, and the tires squealed in protest as the car reversed out of the driveway. Scott threw himself on the ground as the Packard roared by. He caught a glimpse of Twitch hunched over the wheel, and then he was gone.

Scott got up and headed for the woods. Something sure had stirred them up at the farmhouse. . . .

When Twitch gunned the engine, the car threw itself violently over a bump, became airborne, then hit the road again with a whack. The chauffeur's grip on the wheel tightened, but he didn't slow down. His eyes strained ahead. His prisoner had escaped somehow, while they were having dinner, but he couldn't have had much of a head start. Surely the headlights would pick him up before he reached the main road.

The car raced past the inn, and Twitch briefly considered stopping and consulting with Vandam. He dreaded the thought of confronting him with the news; he would bear the brunt of the blame, he knew. He could say that someone must have helped in the escape, but, in the end, he was the one in charge.

Seeing the big red stop sign ahead, he braked, and the car skidded to a halt at the intersection with the highway. An old Chevy pickup rattled by, its lights showing empty highway as far as he could see. The damn kid had probably hitched a ride and was already on his way to Prescott.

He groaned and made a U-turn on the highway.

Back at the inn, Twitch ignored the questioning stare of the night clerk behind the front desk. He headed straight for Vandam's room. Now he'd have to go job-hunting again. He knew how hard that would be, with the way he twitched constantly, jumping at the slightest noise, with his mood swings and uncontrollable temper.

He paused outside Vandam's door to take a deep breath, then he knocked.

Vandam opened the door. His sleeves were rolled up, and a map was spread out on the desk behind him. "Well?"

The chauffeur had trouble getting the words out, his chin twitching. "The kid's gone," he blurted. "I've searched the road."

The blood drained from Vandam's face. "You idiot! How did he get away?"

Twitch shifted uneasily. "I don't know, Mr. Vandam. Someone may have helped him. I think we had a prowler earlier when the dog barked. Maybe it was him."

"Well, don't just stand there like a dummy," Vandam fumed. "Keep looking! No, wait. Get the others first." He grabbed a pencil. "Here's their room numbers. Tell them it's an emergency and to meet me here immediately. Then get back to the car and wait for orders."

"Yes, sir," Twitch said. At least he hadn't been fired on the spot.

They arrived one by one, hurrying into the room with puzzled looks. Vandam shut the door and turned to face them.

"That idiot chauffeur's let the prisoner escape. He knows too much about us, he and that friend of his from the *Rapids Prince*. Now there's nothing to stop them going to the authorities with their story, if we don't collar him before he gets clean away."

There were groans of concern from the group gathered around Vandam.

"Twitch has already searched the road," he said. "But there's still the woods. He could be hiding there, waiting for morning."

Vandam looked at his watch. "Put your warmest clothes on, and meet me out front in ten minutes. We'll split up and comb the woods. There might be time to get him yet."

SIXTEEN

Adam was making slow progress, stumbling over fallen trees and getting tangled up in shrubs that seemed to reach out with clumps of burrs to grab him. He'd lost all sense of direction. He hoped he was headed for the lake, but he could be going in circles for all he knew.

A flurry of snapping branches ahead made him stop short. *Not another one of those night creatures!* He'd already been startled out of his wits by a porcupine – a great prickly thing, standing on its hind legs and chewing on the bark of a tree. It had given him a scornful look and taken its time ambling away, the quills of its lethal tail dragging behind.

The noise ahead stopped, so he carried on, pushing branches out of his way and trampling shrubs, his face and arms scratched and bleeding. Suddenly he caught a glimpse of something moving, off to his right. Something big. *Are there bears here?* His skin prickled, and he hid behind the trunk of a large oak. Whatever it was, he could hear it breathing.

What to do? No use climbing the tree, a bear could easily outclimb him. *Oh, God, now it's coming this way. Closer and closer.* Maybe if he played dead. He closed his eyes, waiting for the mortal blow.

When nothing happened, he opened them again. It was only a few feet from him, staring right at him.

"Adam?" it said.

He peered closer.

"*Scott!* What a relief! How did you get here?"

"I was going to ask you the same thing."

At that moment, they heard a car speed up the road from the inn and screech to a stop amidst the slam of doors. "You two start from here and work your way towards the lake," a voice shouted above the wind. "Walther and I will go on up to the farmhouse and start from there. We'll meet up later."

"It's Vandam and the others!" Scott said. "We'd better get going."

"Which way is the lake?"

Scott pointed south. "That way. Lindsay has a cabin there."

They looked at each other, then plunged ahead as fast as they could.

It started to rain.

———

Lindsay opened the door to the persistent hammering. Vandam was standing there, rain running off his hat, his clothes torn and muddy.

"Sorry to trouble you, miss, but we're searching for a boy who's disappeared. We're concerned he's lost his way in the woods, and we're checking the cabins in case he found shelter in one."

"How old is he, Mr. Dale?" Lindsay asked, remembering to use the name he registered under.

"Sixteen or so." Vandam craned his neck, trying to look past Lindsay into the dimly lit cabin. "You haven't seen him, by any chance?"

Lindsay stayed blocking the doorway. "If he's sixteen, sir, I wouldn't worry too much. I should think he'll turn up soon."

"Are there more cabins around here?"

"There are several between here and the inn."

Vandam gave up trying to see past her. "I'll ask there then. If he does turn up, let me know immediately. It's urgent." He turned away and took the path back to the inn.

Lindsay watched him go, then shut the door and locked it. "He was doing his best to look in," she said. "I think he's suspicious."

Adam's voice came from behind the worn sofa,

which sagged against the far wall. "He doesn't trust anyone, that Vandam."

Scott stuck his head out from behind the kitchen door. "We should head for the ship before he comes back," he said.

"What, tonight?" Lindsay said. "It's a long way, and it's teeming rain."

"I know, but there's no time to waste," Scott said. "We have to tell someone there's a gang of spies here, before they get away."

"Yeah, but who do we tell?" Adam said.

"Start with Captain Plum, I guess."

"Oh, God, do we have to face *him?*" Adam groaned.

When Vandam arrived back at the inn, the others were waiting for him. Their reports were all negative – the captive appeared to have gotten clean away.

Pacing back and forth, Vandam said, "You realize what this means. That kid will find his way to his ship. Then he'll go to the authorities and spill his story."

"But how much does he know?" someone asked.

"Too much," Vandam said. "Unfortunately, his friend overheard me talking to Twitch about Heinrik and our plan to deal with the agent following him – the one who went overboard in the rapids."

"But who will believe them?" someone else asked. "They might think they're just kids making it all up to get attention."

Vandam shook his head. "We can't take the chance. You remember our orders: if any one assignment becomes too risky, it should be abandoned rather than jeopardize the whole mission."

"So what do you propose?"

"I don't propose, I order. I am changing the plan. We have important operations to undertake in the United States. We will cross the border immediately by boat and carry on there until things calm down. This storm will make detection unlikely."

"But if we leave now, what about Operation Blockade?" another wanted to know. "It's key to the war effort."

"We'll come back and tackle that later," Vandam said, "but first we'll make our way to Long Island, in time for the next U-boat drop-off. Has anyone seen Heinrik?"

"He was with us when we were searching for the kid," someone piped up, "but I haven't seen him since. Shall I go look for him?"

"No time. If Heinrik doesn't show up, we'll have to leave without him. He can take care of himself. We can't risk all of us being rounded up here. That would be disastrous.

"I'll speak to the front desk and tell them something's come up and we have to leave immediately. Meet me at the dock. Walther's contact will be there with his boat to take us. It'll be a rough crossing in this weather, but it isn't far. We have to get across before those kids come back with the police, looking for us."

The storm was gaining in intensity as Adam and Scott set out. "Too risky to use the road," Adam said. "Twitch will be on the lookout there. Best to follow the shoreline to Prescott."

"Easier said than done," Scott replied. "But I guess it's the only way."

The first stretches proved to be easy, however, even with the rain and the pounding surf – there were mostly sandy beaches and rows of cottages. Nobody was about at this late hour. Even the dogs were inside, sleeping out the storm.

But they soon had to clamber over rocks and boulders slippery with moss. Lashed by the teeming rain, driven horizontal by the wind, they slid and slithered. Their legs, already scratched from the woods, were bleeding freely, and they were racked with exhaustion as the shoreline stretched ahead of them endlessly.

———

It was almost morning when Adam and Scott finally trudged wearily up the gangway of the *Rapids Prince*. The watchman waved at them from under the shelter of an overhang, making it plain he wasn't about to venture into the open.

They agreed that waking Captain Plum at this hour was out of the question. "It would take more nerve than I have," Adam said. "I'm so beat, I wouldn't make sense anyway."

"Suits me," Scott said. Exhausted, he had to lean against the rail to hold himself up. "Let's get some sleep first."

"It'll be a short sleep – it's practically dawn," Adam grumbled. He made his way to his room, while Scott headed below to the deckhands' quarters in the hold. There, he dumped his sopping-wet clothes on the floor, toweled off, and fell into his bunk.

SEVENTEEN

A few hours later, having dragged himself out of bed, Adam set a plate of bacon and eggs in front of Captain Plum with trepidation. The captain put down his coffee and looked up at him. "So you finally decided to come back to work, young man."

"Yes, sir."

"There have been all sorts of wild rumors going around about your whereabouts. Mind you, I didn't believe half of them. But nobody could tell me exactly where you'd gone, not even your friend. All I could get out of that boy was that you'd be back soon."

"Yes, sir."

"Is that all you've got to say for yourself? Yes, sir?"

"Yes . . . I mean no, sir. You see what happened was —"

Captain Plum held up his hand. "Not while I'm having breakfast. Come to my cabin when I'm finished."

"What's *he* doing here?" the captain said, when he opened the door to Adam's knock and found Scott there, too. "I didn't say anything about bringing him with you."

"No, sir. But Scott was the one they were after, not me."

The captain frowned. "The one who was after? Oh, never mind, you'd better both come in then, but I want the truth, mind, not some long story full of excuses."

"Yes, sir." The two boys filed in and stood uncertainly. Scott took in the captain's quarters, a room he'd never expected to enter during his summer as a lowly deckhand.

A framed map of the St. Lawrence hung on one wall, surrounded by photos of ships – from sleek liners to fat freighters, many emitting dark billows of smoke from their stacks as if proud of this symbol of their might. On the bookshelf, a thick leather-bound Bible propped up a selection of marine manuals. A framed photo of a stout, erect woman, in a black shawl with a severe expression, sat on the desk.

The captain reclined in his chair. "All right, young man, let's have it. Why have you missed two days' work? And be quick about it. I haven't got all day."

Adam took a deep breath and plunged in. "Well, sir, in a nutshell I was kidnapped and held hostage."

The captain shot up from his chair. "I thought I'd heard every excuse in the book. But this is a new one. Held hostage where? By whom?"

"By the man in the gray suit who was on the ship last Sunday, sir," he said, "and his chauffeur. As to where, all I know is I was locked in a room, first somewhere in Old Montreal, then in a farmhouse on the other side of Prescott. I escaped last night with the help of a French Canadian girl, who had befriended me, and –"

Scott saw a purple flush creeping up the captain's face and cringed. *Shut up, Adam,* he thought.

The captain brought his fist down so hard, he knocked over the picture on his desk. "I might have known!" he exclaimed. "It always turns out to be the same old excuse in the end. A young woman."

He quickly set the picture back upright. Maybe it was a mistake for him to hire these students and then turn them loose in Montreal, the city of sin.

Scott saw it was time to intervene. "But, Captain, he really *was* kidnapped. It was the man in the Packard and the men with him. They're Nazis, and they grabbed Adam as a hostage."

The captain frowned at him. "Whatever gave you that idea?"

"I overheard them, sir. When they were sitting in the Packard, parked at the dock in Prescott last Sunday." And Scott proceeded to relate what he had overheard, leaving out the pie-eating part and blaming his abiding interest in the Packard Touring Sedan for being there.

Having gotten over that hurdle successfully, he hurried on to tell the captain how the men had collared Adam as a hostage when the ship arrived in Montreal so he, Scott, wouldn't dare tell what he knew.

To his intense relief, the captain didn't entirely dismiss his account, though he still looked skeptical. "And where are these so-called Nazis now?" he demanded.

"At the Blinkbonnie Inn, just down the road," Adam said, "searching for me since my escape."

At that moment, there was a knock on the door. The captain opened it and found the second mate standing there. "Boat wreckage spotted across the river, Captain," he said. "I thought you'd want to know."

"Wreckage? How big a boat?"

"Hard to say, sir. A motorboat, I think. It must have got caught in the storm last night."

The captain reached for his binoculars. "I'll have a look."

When the second mate saw Scott, he said, "Oh, there you are. I have a message for you. They said it was urgent." He turned to the captain. "There was a young man here earlier – the one who drives for the Blinkbonnie Inn, you know – and he said he had an important message for Scott Graves. I told him to come back later, but he insisted it was urgent. Nobody knew where Scott was, so he gave it to me." He handed an envelope to the captain.

The captain passed it to Scott. "I suppose you'd better open it," he said. "It might be pressing news about your family."

Scott looked at the envelope with hesitation. *What could possibly be so urgent? An accident?* He was conscious of three pairs of eyes fastened on him as he took out the note. But it was from Lindsay, in her neat private-school handwriting: *Thought you should know that Vandam and company checked out suddenly last night. They were last seen boarding a Chris-Craft around midnight.*

"Is it about your father?" the captain said. "Not bad news, I hope?"

"No, sir, it's not about my family." Scott passed him the note. "It's about the Nazi spies. Looks like they've fled across the border by boat. And just when we were about to turn them in!"

The captain skimmed the note, then gave it back. "Well, if there *was* anything to your story, all I can say is good riddance –"

"But, sir," Scott protested, "shouldn't we alert the –"

"That's enough, young man," Captain Plum interrupted sternly. "Just because I'm a friend of your father's doesn't mean you can argue with me. A captain's decision is final, and I've heard all I want to hear about Nazis. It's high time you got back to work. I expect extra effort to make up for all your lost time."

At that, he ushered the boys out, picked up his binoculars, and headed for the bridge. "Now show me this wrecked boat," he said to the second mate.

"What do you bet it's a Chris-Craft?" Scott whispered to Adam.

EIGHTEEN

Scott found out later from Bert, the helmsman, that the captain had indeed identified the wreckage on the U.S. shore as that of a Chris-Craft. The motorboat had apparently been blown aground by the storm. The cabin was still above the water level and clearly visible through binoculars. Uniformed figures were seen at the site.

The occupants, the captain concluded, might have reached land, or they might not have, but the boat was in the U.S. Coast Guard's hands now.

Scott went looking for Adam to tell him the news. He found him working with a polishing rag on a mountain of silverware piled in front of him in the dining room, his hands black with tarnish.

"The steward's given me extra chores to make up for the time I was away," Adam said gloomily. "Chasing a French girl, he claims. Nobody believes us."

"Don't I know it," Scott said.

Adam put down his rag. "I wonder what's happened to Colette? Is she all right? Will I ever see her again?"

Scott tried his best to reassure his friend. "Maybe Twitch drove her back to Montreal in the Packard," he said.

"I wish," Adam said skeptically, just as the steward came in and stood with his hands on his hips, frowning at him.

"You're supposed to be working, not talking to your pal," he said. Adam picked up a gravy boat and began polishing vigorously. Scott slipped out the door, leaving Adam wondering how he could possibly go about finding Colette again.

He would have an opportunity to search for her when the *Rapids Prince* arrived in Montreal after the next excursion. But he had no idea where she lived or even, he realized, what her last name was.

He found that polishing silver, like any repetitive manual work, actually helped him think, and he began to put together a plan. But it would take money, and he hadn't received his first month's pay yet. . . .

———

That evening, Lindsay told Scott what she could about the ill-fated crossing.

"The night porter happened to see them getting into the Chris-Craft around midnight," she said. "He thought it was awfully strange, considering the late hour and the storm, but figured it was none of his business. Then, when I got to work this morning, I heard that the wreckage had been spotted on the American shore. That was when I sent you the note."

"So were they *all* on the Chris-Craft?" Scott asked. "Or just the ones from the Blinkbonnie?"

"He didn't say. But I did see the Packard go by early this morning, when I was on my way to work. It was coming from the farmhouse, so some of them were still there. The chauffeur was driving, and there was a passenger in the back. The car was going so fast, I couldn't tell who it was. That was the last any of us saw of them."

NINETEEN

On the next excursion of the *Rapids Prince,* it was the usual crowd – a busload of seniors, summer-school students, teachers on holiday, families, and honeymoon couples.

Captain Plum was in a good mood. His missing crewman was back on the job, and the inspection had confirmed his ship had suffered only minor damage from the mishap the previous Sunday. He was looking forward to an uneventful trip.

While waiting for the ship to get under way, the purser took some of the passengers on a tour of the ship. He started with the working deck, where he pointed out all the equipment it took to keep the ship in good trim – coils of rope, life jackets, buoys, wooden fenders, paint, cleaners, and other seagoing items. The photographers in the group snapped pictures, with the deckhands posed self-consciously in the background.

One of the photographers, a tall man with a mustache and cap who walked with a limp, appeared to be particularly interested in the ship, snapping pictures wherever he went. He had a miniature camera and carried an expensive-looking leather shoulder bag, loaded with equipment. He asked if they could see the engine room.

The purser shook his head. "Sorry, the chief engineer won't let us down there. Besides, it's hotter than Hades. We'll head up to the bridge next."

The group followed the purser, all except the tall man with the miniature camera. He looked around the working deck, then turned to Scott, who happened to be nearby. "Is that a washroom over there?" he asked.

"It's the crew's washroom," Scott said. "You can use it if you want, but the passenger washrooms on the upper decks are much nicer."

"This one will do just fine, thank you," the tall man said, which left Scott shaking his head.

The rest of the excursion that Sunday finished uneventfully, and the ship pulled into Victoria Pier ahead of schedule. Adam came down from the dining room to see Scott as the deckhands unloaded the luggage.

"Hey, I'm flush again," he said, rattling the change in his pocket. "A bunch of big tippers today."

"Good," Scott said. "Now you can pay me back the three bucks you owe me."

"Don't worry, I will," Adam said. "But would you mind waiting for it? I'm going to look for Colette, and I'll need all the money I can raise to pay the taxi. As a matter of fact, I was hoping you could lend me another fiver."

Scott sighed. "I suppose. At least it's for a good cause. But how are you going to find her again? I never did figure out exactly where the duplex was they took you into."

"Neither did I – I was blindfolded," Adam said. "But I know she works part-time in a library, so that's a start. I'll ask the purser for an advance on my pay, and, with that and your fiver, I can grab a taxi and get going."

Scott couldn't help but admire his nerve. He couldn't imagine asking for an advance on his pay, or spending it all on a taxi. Adam must surely be in love.

By the time Adam got to the pier, there was only one taxi left. But just as he opened the door, a tall man wearing a cap limped up from the ship, jumped in ahead of him, and slammed the door in his face.

"Hey!" Adam said. Passenger or not, he wasn't going to let him get away with that, even if he did have a limp. He rapped on the glass.

The man looked up at him, then turned quickly away. He picked up his cap, which had been knocked off as he got in, and jammed it back on his head. But not before Adam had seen his distinctive blond hair.

"Drive on," the man ordered. The taxi did a U-turn and took off, leaving Adam staring after it, wondering where he had seen the man before. Then it struck him. *It's either Heinrik or someone who looks very much like him! But it can't be. Heinrik crossed the border with the others on the Chris-Craft, didn't he?*

At that moment, another taxi pulled up and Adam got in before anybody else could claim it. Finding Colette was what mattered, and he promptly put the man who looked like Heinrik out of his mind.

«*Parlez-vous anglais?*» he asked the driver.

The driver turned to look at him. "*Un peu*. Where you go?"

Adam made a circle with his hand. «*Le Vieux Montréal.*»

«*Une tournée?*»

"Not exactly. I'm looking for someone, but I don't know her address."

The driver frowned. "Then how we find her?"

"I know she works at a library." Adam searched his brain for the French word. «*Une bibliothèque.*»

«*Ah, une bibliothèque. Ou est-elle?*»

Adam shrugged. «*Dans le Vieux Montréal.*»

The driver seemed to be getting interested in the quest. "Plenty *bibliothèques* in Old Montreal," he said. "But, okay, we try."

He stopped first at an old stone building wedged between a grocery store and a candy shop. «*Une bibliothèque,*» he said.

"Okay," Adam said. "Wait here."

He went in, hoping to see Colette shelving books. When there was no sign of her, he approached the elderly lady at the desk. «*Parlez-vous anglais, madame?*»

"But of course, young man," she said, peering at him sternly over her glasses. "I'm a librarian, what do you expect?"

"*Ah,* pardon my ignorance," Adam apologized. "I'm new here and I need help."

Her gaze softened. "How can I help you?"

"I'm looking for a friend. She works part-time in a library, but I don't know which one. Her name is Colette."

"Colette." She shook her head. "Sorry, no one of that name works here."

Well, it was the first one he'd tried. He waited while the librarian checked out picture books for two young girls, who looked at Adam and giggled.

"Are there other libraries in this part of Montreal?" he asked.

The librarian nodded and wrote down several names and addresses. "You could try these."

Adam got back in the cab and glanced at the meter. He'd managed to squeeze an advance on his pay out of the purser, but it wouldn't last long at this rate. He showed the driver the addresses the librarian had given him.

The next stop also drew a blank, but at the following one, the librarian remembered a Colette who came in sometimes for books. But she didn't work there. "This Colette is a fast reader," the librarian said. "She says she's read everything in the library where she works."

"That's her!" Adam said excitedly. "Did she say which library that was?"

The woman thought for a moment. "St. Margaret's, I believe." She looked up the address for him.

"Good luck," she said as Adam thanked her and rushed out. The meter was ticking.

At St. Margaret's, Adam hurried in and scanned the aisles, but there was no sign of Colette. The woman at the desk said that Colette had worked there part-time, but she'd phoned a few weeks ago to say she was going away for a while and another girl was taking her place.

"Could you give me her home address?" Adam asked.

The woman eyed him. "That would be most irregular," she said.

"Her phone number then?"

She hesitated. "Well, I guess that would be all right."

The taxi driver pulled up beside a phone booth, and Adam put in his nickel and dialed. He waited, praying he would hear Colette's voice.

«*Allô?*» It was her mother.

Pulling out a handkerchief, he covered the receiver. "Could I speak to Colette, *s'il vous plaît?*" he said in a muffled voice. "It's the library. I have a message for her."

"Colette's away."

"When will she be back?"

"She didn't say. Who is this?" she asked suspiciously.

Adam hung up.

Back at the pier, he handed the driver his week's pay.

Will I ever see Colette again? he wondered. *What could have happened to her?*

TWENTY

As the *Rapids Prince* began the return trip to Prescott, Adam was gloomy.

"I was hoping Colette was the other person Lindsay saw leaving in the Packard," he said to Scott. "But I guess she wasn't."

"Too bad Lindsay didn't get a better look," Scott agreed. "But, hey, look on the bright side. Maybe it *was* her."

"Yeah, then why isn't she home yet?"

Having no answer, Scott left to join the other deck-hands to begin cleaning up the ship, readying it for the next load of passengers. Today, the deckhands had a new boss, and Scott didn't want to be late.

Not much older than the deckhands he was now in charge of, the new boss, Charles, seemed older. Rumor had it he'd been with the army overseas, where he'd lost an arm below the elbow. Recovered from his wounds, he'd been honorably discharged back to Canada.

According to Bert, the helmsman and fountain of information, Charles had been a deckhand for a summer before the war. When he applied for his old job back, Captain Plum readily agreed, putting him in charge of the new student deckhands.

Now they were hard at work, scrubbing the decks for the next boatload of passengers to mess up. Watching Charles handle the hose, Scott marveled at how he was able to do as much with one arm as anyone else with two. He longed to ask him how he'd lost his arm, but thought Charles wouldn't want to talk about it.

Mickey, one of the other deckhands, wasn't so reticent. "Where were you when you were wounded?" he asked.

When Charles turned on the hose and began wetting down the deck, Scott thought he wasn't going to answer. "Dieppe," he finally said, in a clipped voice.

"Dieppe was the raid on Europe where everything went wrong for the Canadians, wasn't it?" Mickey said.

"That's about the size of it," Charles answered.

"How come?" Mickey persisted.

Charles looked at him. "If you'd stop using that

brush as a leaning post and start scrubbing with it, I'll tell you."

Mickey jumped to it, and Charles was as good as his word. "It was a mess from the start," he began. "The raid had to be a surprise to succeed, but a patrol boat spotted our flotilla crossing the Channel. The Germans were ready for us. Just waiting."

Charles stared at the canal. "It should have been canceled right then, or at least postponed, but Lord Mountbatten went ahead and ordered the troops in. Crazy. The shells were already bursting around us before our landing craft even got close to the beach. Half our guys were killed while we were still in deep water."

"Jeez," Mickey said, "and they never even made it to the beach?"

"Some beach!" Charles snorted. "More like an obstacle course – mostly pebbles polished by the sea. That was another thing the generals back in London forgot to tell us. You couldn't run on the stuff, and our tanks just sat there, churning, the pebbles stuck in their tracks. We made easy targets."

He turned the hose full blast on a nearby post as if it were one of those generals who sent them into this trap.

"Somehow I managed to make it to the shelter of a retaining wall. When I looked back, the German machine guns were having a field day. All I could see were bodies and burnt-out tanks. I recognized my best friend – his legs were missing. I would have gone back to help him, but I could tell he was dead." Charles' voice cracked.

Scott concentrated on obliterating a stubborn smudge on the deck, trying to dispel the grisly image.

After a moment, Charles continued, "Only a few of us managed to get back to the boats – that was when my arm was shattered by machine-gun bullets. But I am one of the lucky ones – I'm still alive. Most of the others were either dead or pinned down on the beach and had to surrender. I was with *Les Fusiliers Mont-Royal*, and we were one of the hardest hit. Of six hundred men, only a hundred and twenty-five of us made it back to England."

There was silence.

Finally Mickey piped up, "Guess they'll never try that again, eh? The generals, I mean."

Charles bent down to straighten out the kinks in the hose. "Oh, they will soon enough. They have to, otherwise we'll never liberate Europe. But the next landing will be different. I guess that's what Dieppe came down to in the end – a learning experience. Even generals learn from their mistakes."

Scott looked around. Everyone was busy scrubbing, heads down. *We're probably all wondering the same thing,* he thought. *How would we have done if we'd been the ones hitting that beach? Which we might well do in a few years' time. But the way things are going in the Pacific, it might be a Japanese beach.*

Until now, he couldn't wait to join up. He still would, when the time came, but now he realized there was another side to war, not just adventure, the companionship of buddies, and the glamour of a uniform.

TWENTY-ONE

Colette was getting restless. It had been almost a week since they'd left the farmhouse in a rush and driven to the safe house, on a remote road north of Montreal. And Vandam still hadn't shown up.

"I guess he isn't coming," she said. "I'd like to go home, Tyler. There isn't even a phone here to call my mother. Can you drive me?"

"Not yet," Twitch said. He wasn't ready to give up. He'd heard the Chris-Craft cabin was found intact on the other shore and suspected his boss had survived. But he had no idea what Vandam's plans were. Keep your mouth shut and obey orders was his credo. At least he hadn't been fired for letting the prisoner escape.

For all Twitch knew, Vandam and the others were lying low in the United States until it was safe to come back. Then they'd finish what they had set out to do in Canada. "Wait a few more days," he said to Colette.

He took a dish of food out for the guard dog and watched him gobble it up. "Good, eh, Pierre?" he said. He'd grown quite fond of the dog, not like at first, when he would drop the food in front of the dog and hurry back to the shelter of the farmhouse.

He wondered how long he could hold off taking the girl home. Once she told her mother what Vandam was up to, there'd be trouble. They might even go to the police.

And what was he supposed to do with the Packard? *Vandam and his high living! He couldn't use an ordinary car, say a Ford or a Chevy. Oh, no, it had to be a fancy Packard Twelve Touring Sedan.* "It's part of my image as a wealthy patriot," he remembered Vandam saying.

Before he got the job with Vandam, Twitch had been driving for the kingpin of a Montreal mob in the protection racket. It was a job he'd drifted into during the Depression, after losing his job as a security guard at the bank and searching in vain for similar work. Then, when the mobster he drove for was gunned down, he got hired by Vandam.

He knew Vandam was into something shady, too, and eventually came to realize what he and his followers were up to. He didn't like it, but it was a job.

Lately, however, he'd begun to wonder if it was worth it. *If it turns out they are planning to do real damage to the country's war effort,* he told himself, *I'll quit this business. My loyalty belongs to Canada, not to a bunch of Nazis.*

When Pierre polished off his dish of food, Twitch reached down and stroked his head before returning to the house. Just as he reached the back door, the dog suddenly barked. He stopped and listened, aware of the dog's supersensitive hearing.

It wasn't long before he heard a car approaching. He tensed. The road was rarely used – there was just one other house and, after that, a dead end. He went around to the front to see who it was.

The car appeared in a swirl of dust. It was a taxi, and the passenger in the back stared at him as it went by. That made him uneasy. He watched until the taxi briefly disappeared around a bend. A few minutes later, it came back, empty.

Twitch had been told the house at the end of the road was unoccupied. He didn't like the way the passenger had stared at him, so he lingered outside.

Soon a figure appeared on the road. The weather had cooled, and the rising mist and the rapidly descending darkness gave the approaching figure a phantomlike appearance. A phantom that walked with a limp. It came on, ignoring the barking dog. Twitch tensed and his hand tightened on his gun.

The figure stopped at the end of the driveway. "Hello, Twitch."

The man had dusky skin and a mustache, and he wore a cap. Taking off one of his shoes, he shook out a pebble. "Hurts a bit, and it's guaranteed to make you limp," he said. "A pebble in the shoe, I mean."

Twitch shifted nervously.

"Still don't recognize me? It's the skin dye and the mustache; the limp helps, too. Simple stuff, but it works. I was taught that in spy school, back in Germany. I didn't have time to dye my hair, so I bought this to cover it." He took off his cap, revealing his blond hair.

"Heinrik!" Twitch exclaimed. "I wondered who it was in the taxi. But why didn't you get off here?"

"I didn't want the driver to know where I was staying, so I had him drop me at the other house. I walked back – I can't be too careful. What are my chances for a meal? I haven't eaten all day. I was too busy on board the *Rapids Prince*."

"Come on in," Twitch said. "Colette will cook something for you."

In the kitchen, Colette fried some sausages and potatoes while Heinrik and Twitch talked in the living room. She hadn't recognized Heinrik at first either, until she took a closer look at those pale blue eyes and that tall lean build. Then, when he took his cap off, his hair gave him away.

Apparently his disguise had worked on the *Rapids Prince,* too, judging from what he was saying now. She strained to hear more.

"Vandam panicked," he said. "He abandoned Operation Blockade and fled across the border when the hostage escaped. But I'm not one to flee at the first sign of trouble. I stayed to carry out my mission."

Twitch said something about the risk he'd taken by boarding the *Rapids Prince* a second time, when there were many other ships that used the canal.

"Yes, but they're freighters that take only cargo," Heinrik said. "That's why the *Rapids Prince* is so important to us. She takes passengers – as long as you've got money you can book a passage, no questions asked. So I disguised myself for the second trip.

"Mission accomplished, in any case," he went on. "It's just a matter of time now. The *Rapids Prince*'s days are numbered. And when she goes down, she'll take Allied shipping down with her."

Colette's blood ran cold.

"But I'll be far away by the time that happens.

There'll be a heck of a fuss over here. RCMP all over the place. I'd suggest you make yourself scarce, too, Twitch."

TWENTY-TWO

Adam was leaning on the rail, watching the world go by and dreaming about Colette. They were steaming up the Soulanges Canal, en route back to Prescott. It was an easy time for him – no passengers to look after, only the officers to wait on.

The ship's whistle let out a blast, making him jump. An approaching freighter gave a return blast and churned by, with only a few feet to spare in the narrow canal. The freighters were loaded with essential supplies – iron ore from Lake Superior, guns and tanks for the armies overseas, grain and beef to feed those armies.

Cars were going by on the highway, which ran alongside the canal. A family, picnicking on the grass, waved at Adam. As did a girl in a car traveling in the same direction as the ship. He waved back casually, but when she kept on waving and gesturing, he looked more closely.

With a start, he realized the car was the Packard Twelve Touring Sedan and the girl . . . *can it be?* He peered . . . *yes, it's her!*

Adam waved frantically, jumping up and down in his excitement. The driver – he recognized Twitch at the wheel now – slowed down enough for the car to keep abreast of the ship.

Colette was pointing ahead. *What is she trying to tell me?* Scott would know.

He clambered down to the working deck where the deckhands were gathered, ready to moor the ship at the next lock.

Scott caught his friend's frantic gesturing and came over. "Hey, what's up, Adam?"

"It's Colette!" Adam could hardly contain himself. "She's here!"

"She is?" Scott looked around. "Where?"

"No, no, not here. There."

"You're not making sense," Scott said. "Calm down."

Adam pointed toward the canal bank and grabbed his arm. "Come and see."

On the deck above, he led Scott to the starboard rail. "There. In the Packard. See?" He stood back, beaming.

Scott looked. *He's gone bananas from worrying about Colette,* he thought as he watched an old Model T Ford go by.

"I hate to tell you this, Adam, but that's not the Packard."

"What?" Adam looked. "That's not the car. Colette was there, Scott, I swear! In the Packard, with Twitch at the wheel."

"You sure?"

"Positive. She kept waving and pointing ahead, as if they were going somewhere and she wanted me to meet her there. What's up ahead?"

"The first lock. It's a mile or two yet."

"Then that must be what she meant," Adam said. "She'll meet us at the lock. Just wait, you'll see. I'm not crazy."

Adam paced the deck. "Are we nearly there?" he asked for the third time, like a kid on a car trip.

"Patience. Won't be long now," Scott said.

Presently, the throb of the ship's engines stopped, and the *Rapids Prince* slowed to a crawl. "There's a ship in the lock," Scott said, "and another waiting in line. We'll have to wait our turn."

"Blast," Adam said. "You mean we have to sit here in the middle of the canal?"

"No, there's a dock where we can tie up while we wait," Scott said. "I have to go below now to get ready."

As the ship glided towards the dock, Scott prepared to jump at just the right moment. He was used to it now – too soon and you risked falling in between the ship and the dock; too late and the ship drifted away.

The instant the *Rapids Prince* nudged the dock, Scott leapt off and ran to catch the lightweight line that Charles threw him from the bow. He hauled on it until the heavy mooring line it was attached to appeared, like a monster from the deep. Dragging it to the nearest post, he dropped the loop over it. Charles winched in the line until the bow was secured.

Not till all the lines were similarly secured did Scott have time to pause and look around. The first thing he saw was the Packard, parked across the road, Colette getting out, and Adam leaping ashore. A shout stopped him cold.

"Ahoy, you there!" It was Captain Plum from the bridge. "No one's allowed ashore here except deckhands. Get yourself back on board this minute!"

Adam hesitated, then grabbed Colette's hand. "I can't stay. Come over here and talk to me." He led her to the ship, then, aware of the captain glaring down at him, jumped back on board. "I've been looking all over Montreal for you," he said. "I'm so glad you're safe."

"I've been wondering about you too," Colette said. "I'm happy you got back to your ship all right, after your escape. But there is something important I have to tell you –"

"I hope they didn't blame you for my escape," Adam interrupted.

"No, Vandam blamed poor Tyler, which isn't fair, but, Ad*am*, something else has happened that –"

"Vandam? I thought he'd left in the Chris-Craft!"

Colette stamped her foot. "Ad*am*! Listen to me. Heinrik says your ship will . . . how you say? . . . explode. You must *do* something."

"Explode? Heinrik said that?"

"He admitted to Twitch that his mission was to blow up a ship in a lock and block the canal. So he planted a bomb. Twitch told me he'd bring me here, but I would have to do the talking. He used to drive for the Mafia and won't have anything to do with the authorities."

Scott couldn't help overhearing. "Good Lord, a bomb!"

"Yes, and you must find it," Colette urged. "Before it's too late."

Adam and Scott exchanged looks. "The captain," they both said, and they stared up at the bridge, where Captain Plum was glowering down at the girl who was keeping his crew from their duties.

"You go," Adam said.

"No, you go. I have to stay on the dock and take care of the lines."

"Do something," Colette urged. "Quickly."

At that moment, Charles appeared. "What's going on with you guys? You heard the captain. Get back to your posts."

"But Colette says a bomb's been planted on the ship," Adam protested.

"What!"

"A bomb. Planted by a German agent."

Charles' expression hardened. "If you're pulling my leg . . ."

"He isn't, I swear," Scott chimed in. "Colette says Heinrik –"

"Hold on a minute," Charles interrupted. "Who's this Heinrik, and who is Colette?"

«*Je suis Colette,*» Colette said.

Charles looked across the gap at the girl standing on the bank. «*Eh bien!*» he said and immediately launched into rapid-fire French neither Adam nor Scott could follow.

Charles and Colette talked at length until Charles finally turned to them. "Hard to believe," he said, "but Colette's story sounds genuine. It's possible this Heinrik *could* have planted a bomb on board yesterday."

"I'm glad you got it directly from Colette," Adam

said. "I had no idea someone named Charles would speak French like a native."

"Ever heard of Charles de Gaulle?" Charles said curtly. "I *am* French. But never mind that. There's no time to waste if there's a bomb timed to explode in the lock! I'm going to see the captain right now and recommend an immediate search of the ship."

"But I must warn you," said Adam, "the captain will be hard to convince. I tried to tell him about the Nazis before, but he seemed to think I made it up to excuse missing work last week, especially when he heard there was a girl involved."

"Maybe so," Charles said, "but I certainly don't intend to sit here and do nothing. In my opinion, we should call in the RCMP and have the ship searched by professionals. I've been through enough explosions already in this war."

TWENTY-THREE

In the lock, an eastbound freighter was slowly sinking to their level. There was one other westbound ship waiting at the dock, ahead of the *Rapids Prince*. When that ship entered the lock and was raised, it would be their turn next. And time was passing.

Scott looked up at the bridge, where Charles was talking to the captain. It looked like he was having a hard time convincing him. The captain stared balefully at Colette on the dock and at Twitch in the Packard across the road.

Scott was beginning to sweat. There was the entire ship to search!

Finally, Charles left the bridge. Arriving below, he looked perturbed. "The captain doesn't put much stock in this business. He's not about to call in the RCMP based on what a teenage girl and a chauffeur tell us. It will make him look a fool when they don't find anything. He thinks we're getting all worked up over nothing."

"You mean, we've got to sit here and wait to see if the ship blows up?" cried Adam.

"We're not going to do that," Charles said. "The three of us can search the ship. We haven't got long until it's our turn in the lock. Where's a likely place to hide something so it won't be noticed – even if it's ticking?"

They were silent, each one mentally going over the ship.

"The lifeboats!" Scott said suddenly. "They're hardly ever used, and they're covered, so a bomb wouldn't be seen."

"Of course!" Charles said. They rushed up the stairs to the upper deck, drawing curious glances from the other crew members.

"I'll start here," Charles said, undoing the catches that fastened the canvas cover on the first lifeboat. "You guys take the next two. If you see anything suspicious, don't touch it."

They searched each lifeboat carefully, peering under the seats, unstrapping the life preservers, and opening the emergency-rations containers. *Nothing.*

From the upper deck, they had a good view of the lock. Scott could see that the gates were open and the freighter ahead of them was entering. It was their turn next.

"The lifeboats are clean," Charles said. "Where are the other places Heinrik could hide a bomb?"

"There's the dining room, of course," Adam said. "But the steward would have a fit if we went in there and messed it up."

"I'll go talk to him," Charles said.

He must have put a scare into the steward, because the next thing Scott and Adam knew, they were called in and told they could search anywhere they wanted.

They peered under the tables, behind the drapes, and in the cupboards, hauling out any serving dishes large enough to accommodate a bomb. *Again, nothing.*

They searched the lounge and behind the stacked deck chairs. *Still nothing.*

"Now what?" Charles said. "No point in searching the engine room – that's the chief engineer's domain and he never allows passengers down there. That leaves only the lower deck, but you guys are usually around down there. We're running out of options." He lowered his voice. "I don't doubt that Colette is telling the truth, but I'm beginning to think that Heinrik may be playing tricks on us."

"How do you mean?" Adam said.

"Maybe he wasn't even here. Maybe he planted the rumor but not the bomb. Then we'd do a thorough search, but when we don't find anything, we would treat the next scare as just another false alarm."

"But he was here. I know, I saw him getting in the taxi," Adam said.

"But are you sure it was him you saw?"

"Pretty sure. He was in disguise, but I saw his blond hair when his cap fell off. And it's easy to fake a limp, and he was as tall as Heinrik and –"

"Wait a minute," Scott interrupted. "You say he was tall and had a limp? Then he *was* here!"

"He was?"

"Yes, but I didn't recognize him. The purser took some of the passengers on a tour, and he brought them down here. When they left, a man, just like the one you described, didn't go along with them."

"What did he do then?" Charles asked.

Scott pointed to the crew's washroom. "He went in there."

"The crew's washroom?" Charles said incredulously. "But it's so tiny, you can hardly turn around. Where could you hide a bomb in there?"

"The toilet tank?" Scott suggested.

They dashed for the washroom so quickly that Scott and Adam got tangled in the doorway.

"Wait, let me look," Charles said. They stood back. Charles entered and cautiously lifted the lid on the toilet tank. He peered in. "There it is, all right! It's taped to the inside of the tank." He stood back to let Scott and Adam look.

"Wow! Look at that! But how do we get rid of it? Throw it overboard?"

"If you touch it the wrong way, it can detonate," Charles warned. "I'm not fooling with it – that's a job for a bomb-disposal expert."

"I can hear it ticking," Scott said.

"The whole ship should be evacuated immediately," Charles announced. "Once the captain sees it, I'm sure he'll agree. In the meantime, don't let anyone near it. Thank God we found it!"

TWENTY-FOUR

They'd never seen the captain move so fast. He came shooting down the stairs, stared at the device for a moment, then raced back up, not saying a word.

"He's not taking any chances," Charles said, when he returned from the bridge. "We're to evacuate the ship immediately, and he's getting the RCMP to come and dispose of the bomb. Until they get here, the ship won't budge from the dock."

"But Heinrik couldn't have known what time the *Rapids Prince* would reach the first lock, could he?" Scott asked Charles, as they waited by the side of the road with the rest of the crew. "So how could he have set the timer on his bomb?"

"He probably asked questions when he was on

board Sunday," Charles said. "And even if his timing wasn't dead-on and the bomb went off too soon, or too late, and sank the ship in the canal, it would still block shipping for a while. Not for as long as a badly damaged lock would, though."

Scott turned to stare at the ship, picturing her blown to smithereens. He imagined the thoughts running through the crew's minds – some lamenting the end of their summer jobs; others more concerned about the loss of ammunition, food, and essential supplies for the Allied armies; still others worried about their personal effects, and the captain about the loss of his command.

In the distance came the faint wail of a siren. As soon as Twitch heard it, he started up the Packard and sped away, tires squealing. "Will he come back to drive you home, Colette?" Adam wondered aloud.

She shook her head. "I think we've seen the last of Tyler now that the RCMP is involved. But I can take a bus back to Montreal, once I'm sure you're safe."

The siren became louder. A van raced up and the bomb-disposal expert got out with his equipment. Charles led him on board and showed him where the bomb was.

"Looks like a powerful one," the man said calmly. "You'd best clear out before I get to work."

Charles waited tensely with the rest of the crew by the road. As the minutes ticked by, the suspense mounted. "Does anyone remember a man asking questions about the ship during the trip to Montreal yesterday?" he asked, mainly to divert their attention.

"What did he look like?" someone wanted to know.

"A tall dark man with a cap," Scott said. "He had a mustache, and . . . oh, yes, he took a lot of pictures."

"Hey, I remember him!" Bert, the helmsman, said. "He came up to me and asked how long it took the *Rapids Prince* to reach the first lock on our return trip. I thought it was an unusual question, but tourists are a curious bunch, so I –" He paled suddenly. "Good Lord, you don't mean to say I helped a Nazi!"

"Don't worry," Charles said, patting his shoulder. "If you hadn't answered him, someone else would have."

"Look!" Scott said, as the man they had all been waiting for appeared on the gangway, gingerly carrying the defused bomb. He placed it in the van, and it drove carefully away, the entire ship's crew cheering it on.

"Well, that's that," the captain said. "Let's get back to work."

Everyone headed for the ship, except Adam, who hung back to be with Colette. "Can we meet when the *Rapids Prince* docks next Sunday?" he asked anxiously.

"Of course –" she began, before being interrupted by a shout.

"Ahoy there, you!"

Adam looked around. It was the captain, gesturing to him. "*Uh-oh,* what have I done now?" he said.

"You two are to proceed to the ship's dining room immediately," the captain said, "along with your friend Scott. I have instructed the steward to lay on a first-class dinner for the three of you, white tablecloth and all."

Adam was too stunned to respond. For a moment, he thought the captain was going to apologize for doubting them. Until Colette turned down his offer.

"Thank you, Captain, that is very thoughtful," she said, "but I really must go home now to let my mother know I'm all right."

The captain colored. Used to being obeyed without question, he managed to restrain himself. "I'll arrange it for our next trip to Montreal then," he said, and turned away.

"Well, that was almost as good as an apology," Adam whispered, as he reached for Colette's hand.

Watching, Scott imagined how surprised their French teacher would be when she found that Adam, whose only interest before had been science, was suddenly eager to learn French.

Not the only surprising event, that unforgettable summer of 1943.

The End

AFTERWORD

It is a matter of record that German agents were put ashore in Canada from U-boats during World War II on at least three separate occasions.

On April 25, 1942, the first agent landed in New Brunswick from U-213 with radio equipment and made his way to Montreal. He was apprehended in 1944.

The second landed from U-518 on November 9, 1942, on the Gaspé Peninsula. He was arrested immediately, confessed, and became a double agent.

The third landing, from U-537, was on October 23, 1942, in northern Labrador. A weather station was set up and remained undetected until after the war.

In the United States, German agents landed near Jacksonville, Florida, and on Long Island, New York, equipped with explosives and large sums of money.

Intent on sabotage, none of their forays was successful.

In this story, the characters, including the German agents and the captain and crew of the *Rapids Prince,* are fictional. What is not fictional, however, is the *Rapids Prince* herself, on which the author served. The ship regularly challenged the Long Sault until the St. Lawrence Seaway, built after the war, drowned the rapids.